William Buell Sprague, Anne Pratt

The Excellent Woman as described in the book of Proverbs

SALZWASSER
VERLAG

William Buell Sprague, Anne Pratt

The Excellent Woman as described in the book of Proverbs

Reprint of the original, first published in 1863.

1st Edition 2022 | ISBN: 978-3-37500-367-8

Verlag (Publisher): Salzwasser Verlag GmbH, Zeilweg 44, 60439 Frankfurt, Deutschland
Vertretungsberechtigt (Authorized to represent): E. Roepke, Zeilweg 44, 60439 Frankfurt, Deutschland
Druck (Print): Books on Demand GmbH, In de Tarpen 42, 22848 Norderstedt, Deutschland

THE

EXCELLENT WOMAN

AS DESCRIBED IN THE

BOOK OF PROVERBS.

WITH AN INTRODUCTION

Embellished with numerous Illustrations engraved by Baker.

BOSTON:

1863.

INTRODUCTION.

We hail it as one of the signs of good, that the female sex have, in these latter years, been gradually coming up to the position of dignity and influence which Providence has evidently designed for them. If we compare woman as she was with woman as she is, or if we view her as she is now under Pagan and under Christian influences, we cannot resist the conviction that Christianity is the wonder-working agent that has produced the change in both her character and her condition. And we have a right to expect that this change will become yet more deep and universal. We anticipate the time when Christianity will dispense to her still brighter glories; when her intellect will act more vigorously, and her heart be lifted up in purer and nobler aspirations; when she will not only better understand, but more faithfully fulfil, her allotted mission; — in short, when her influence shall be felt everywhere, welcomed everywhere, pure as the breath of the morning, and merciful, yet powerful, as the ministry of angels.

But notwithstanding the favorable change that has already taken place, and the yet more favorable change which is justified to our hopes and expectations, it must be acknowledged that we have little reason to be satisfied with the present standard of female excellence, even in those communities where the standard is the highest. Many examples, indeed, there are of female character, which would seem to us to have been formed after a perfect model, and to leave as little to be desired as consists with the present state of human imperfection; but these examples, instead of indicating the ordinary measure of female attainment and usefulness, are always marked as glorious exceptions; they stand forth from the mass in goodly prominence, showing at once what woman may become, and what every woman ought to aspire to, as she would accomplish her legitimate destiny or attain to the highest dignity of her sex.

There is, perhaps, nothing that stands more radically in the way of female progress than that spirit of self-indulgence which so extensively pervades the higher classes of female society. It cannot be disguised that it seems to have become almost an essential part of the economy of fashionable life, that a lady should have little or nothing to do. She may, indeed, make her own toilet; she may, when it is convenient, and she does not wish to spend the hour in sleep, receive the calls of her friends; she may walk in her garden, and admire the progress of vegetation, and be regaled with the fragrance of flowers; she may occasionally take an airing in pleasant weather, and spend here and there a few moments of idle chit-chat with some of her acquaintances; she may grace the splendid ball-room or the fashionable party; she may sometimes even sport a little delicate needle-work with which to adorn in a higher degree her own person; — but further than this she does not go, — much further than this she is forbidden to go, by the false code of fashion to which she has subjected herself. Not that all these things which we have mentioned are in themselves worthy of condemnation; — we would allow to a lady her delicate occupations and her innocent amusements, — but we would not allow her to feel as if these were the greater concerns of human life, — in other words, as if she had nothing to do which did not terminate ultimately in self-indulgence. The truth is, that woman, as well as man, is made for activity; she is gifted with the same intellectual and moral faculties; and though Providence has assigned to her a different sphere of action, yet he has in no wise absolved her from the obligation to be active. Let her remember, then, if she settles down into a state of indolent inaction, because either an opulent condition in life or the false maxims of the age permit it, that she offends as well against the claims of Heaven as against the dignity of her own nature.

But it is not enough that woman should be active; her activity must be guided by discretion and animated by benevolence; she must be contented to work within her own sphere, and to occupy her own quiet throne. It is not more certain that she is endowed with faculties that qualify her for useful exertion, than that she has her own peculiar field of labor indicated to her. But, unhappily, she has not always been satisfied to keep within the bound which the finger of Providence has manifestly drawn around her. She has sometimes forgotten her native modesty, and thrust herself into the rough and tumultuous scenes of life, where her voice has been heard, not to allay, but to swell the tempest. She has talked extravagantly and violently of her own rights, — mistaking a frenzied ambition to be known and heard and talked about, for an honest desire to reform and purify society. And even where she has stopped short of this extreme point, against which all decency and all common sense remonstrate, she has not unfrequently overstepped the bounds of strict decorum, by an interference with matters not appropriately belonging to her. Who, for instance, could hear a lady, at a large dinner-party, making her voice heard above the voices of a dozen professed politicians, in debating some party question, without feeling that she had forgotten her sex and her place, and that no more fitting word of counsel could be addressed to her than that she should remember that she is a woman?

What, then, *is* woman's peculiar sphere? In what field may her influence be most appropriately and most advantageously exerted?

First of all, surely, in her own dwelling — in the sacred privacy of home. Here she sustains her most intimate relations; and the duties belonging to them are sufficient to put in requisition the full vigor of her faculties. What important duties devolve upon her in the relation of a *wife!* Not only is she bound to study the happiness of her husband, — to do what she can to alleviate his burdens of care, and prevent the occasions of disquietude, — but she should consider herself pledged to the promotion of his usefulness in the highest possible degree; and the heart of an affectionate and intelligent wife will quickly find out many means of doing this which nothing but experience could suggest. Hence it has almost grown into a proverb, that an individual who has been eminently successful in business, or eminently useful in society, has been blessed with an uncommonly prudent and excellent wife. In respect to no profession, perhaps, is this remark so frequently or so justly made, as the clerical: almost every minister's standing and general influence are affected more or less by the character of his wife; and while many owe to this circumstance a greatly-increased usefulness, many others find in it a mill-stone about their necks, — their efforts are in a great degree paralyzed, and life with them is little more than a protracted and unbroken sickness of the heart. As a *mother*, too, who shall fix a limit to woman's responsibility? In her house, and under her eye, are growing up the component parts of society in the next generation; and, moreover, each of them has an immortal nature, in which are bound up elements of character that will prove the seeds of an eternal harvest of glory or woe. The father has, indeed, important duties to perform towards these rising immortals: but it is the mother's plastic hand that chiefly forms their characters; it is her winning voice especially that is to make them familiar with the lessons of truth and wisdom; it is her gentle hand that is to lead them into the paths of virtue; it is her firm but loving look in which they are to find the most powerful dissuasive from evil; — in short, it is through her agency, far more than any other, that they are to be formed for a life of honorable usefulness, and an interminable career of virtue and happiness beyond the grave. Is there anything that can task woman's energies and affections, if this does not? But yet another of her domestic relations is that of a *sister*. Suppose her to be the elder of a circle of brothers and sisters — how much is it in her power to do for the improvement and the happiness of all of them! How can she make herself felt by all, not merely in inculcating the maxims of prudence and kindness, nor yet merely in acting as a teacher to those whose faculties are less developed than her own, but in the strict propriety of her daily walk, and by a thousand insensible and nameless influences which become that tender and beautiful relation! It may safely be said, then, that woman is most in her element when she is at home. The objects that meet her eye every hour are those upon which her influence is primarily to be exerted, and through which she is to reach out into the great world.

But, though home is woman's highest and most peculiar sphere, it is by no means her only sphere; she has important work to perform outside of her own dwelling. It is a conceded fact that Heaven has strung in woman's heart a chord that vibrates quickly and deeply to the notes of sorrow, and thus has indicated to her that her mission is to be in no small degree a mission of sympathy and charity. Hence, it is peculiarly fitting that she should make herself at home in the dwellings of the destitute and the desolate; that she should familiarize herself to scenes of mourning, as a comforter to the sorrowful; that she should look after the poor widow and the helpless orphan, making provision for the supply of the one and the education of the other; — in short, that wherever she sees a cup of bitterness administered to a human being, she should endeavor, if it is in her power, to infuse into it some ingredients of consolation. Who does not honor the name of Mrs. Fry, who spent many of her last years in laboring to enlighten and reform the miserable tenants of Newgate? And who does not equally honor our own distinguished countrywoman, Miss Dix, who, with the spirit of a Howard animating every pulsation of her heart, may be said almost literally to be living in prisons, not merely for the physical relief, but for the moral and spiritual benefit, of those whom neither justice nor safety would suffer to be at large?

Nor is it required of woman that she should limit her benevolent offices to scenes of visible and palpable suffering; she may do much, she ought to do much, in sustaining and advancing the interests of true Christianity. She is by no means to be considered as infringing the province of the other sex, or as recreant to the delicacy of her own nature, when she puts forth vigorous and combined efforts for extending the knowledge and influence of the Gospel. We have nothing to say against, but much to say in favor of, female societies in the different departments of evangelical charity: and it is to be devoutly hoped and confidently expected, that with the gradual progress of the spirit of benevolence in future years and ages, these societies will form a far more effective and extended agency than they now do, in the great work of renovating the world.

There is yet another department in which female effort may very properly be encouraged, and in which many females have already labored in a manner worthy of all praise — namely, the department of authorship. There is no reason suggested by delicacy, or common sense, or public sentiment, why a lady who has fine thoughts on any subject of importance, and has the power of expressing them on paper in a fitting manner, should not give them to the world; and hence it has come to pass, especially in latter years, that many of the books which are fitted to exert the most benign influence on society are from female writers. It would be easy to make out a list of such works, not only from the dead but from the living, which have already acquired the character of standard productions, and the loss of which would make a chasm in our literature which it would be hard to realize, and still harder to supply. There are certain subjects upon which females write far more effectively than men; and that must be a dull book, indeed, written by a lady, which the men will not read. Let our gifted ladies, then, not be afraid to use the pen; but let them use it in such a manner that they shall never have occasion to blush for what they have written.

It is an obvious deduction, from the preceding train of thought, that nothing is more important to the well being of society and the prospects of the race, than a high standard of female education; by which I mean, not merely great proficiency in what are commonly called accomplishments, nor even a thorough training of the intellect alone, — but such a formation of the physical, intellectual, moral and social habits, as shall best subserve the great end of a happy and useful life. It scarcely need be said that such a result is not to be looked for, independently of the influence of Christianity; and hence anything that falls short of a Christian education, however it may furnish a passport to the favor of the world, leaves the greatest interests of the present, and all the interests of the future, utterly unprovided for. A female may undoubtedly be amiable in her disposition and attractive in her manners, and may be admired and loved by large circles of friends, while yet she has not the fear of God before her eyes, nor the love of God in her heart; but, in order to fulfil the great end of her existence on earth, and to be prepared for a nobler existence in heaven, she must draw her motives of action from the future and the invisible, and never lose sight of her relations to God and eternity.

Whoever makes a discreet and well-directed effort to improve and elevate the character of woman, is certainly to be regarded as a benefactor to his race. On this ground, I hesitate not to say that the author of the following work has richly merited such a distinction. In a simple and beautiful commentary on Solomon's description of a virtuous woman, we find much light thrown upon the text, by a reference to ancient usages; a fine illustration of various points of difference between the Jewish and the Christian woman; and many of the soundest maxims of wisdom bearing upon the subject of female education. It is a work that will bear to be read more than once; and each successive reading will be likely to reveal some new gem of thought which in the general mass of excellence had been overlooked before. It is a book suitable for the husband to present to his wife, the mother to her daughter, and the brother to his sister; and the more widely it is circulated, the better for the country and the world.

W. B. S.

CONTENTS,

AND

SUBJECTS ILLUSTRATED.

PROVERBS XXXI. 10—31.

WHO CAN FIND
A VIRTUOUS WOMAN!
FOR HER PRICE
IS FAR ABOVE RUBIES.

THE

EXCELLENT WOMAN.

SECTION I.

WHO CAN FIND A VIRTUOUS WOMAN? FOR HER PRICE IS FAR ABOVE RUBIES.

The whole of this beautiful description of female excellence consists of twenty-two verses, distinct from the remaining part of the chapter, and forming, in themselves, a poem, of which each verse commences with a letter of the Hebrew alphabet. It is the conclusion of that book which has been called the storehouse of practical wisdom; and, like the preceding chapters of Proverbs, it is admirable for its just delineations of character, its wise practical directions, and its apt commendations and reproof. To the female sex, in all ages, it presents many striking and valuable lessons. To the Hebrews, indeed, accustomed to a highly figurative mode of discourse, and a perpetual reference to proverbs and wise sayings, the various portions of this book seem singularly appropriate; and perhaps many of those holy women of old, of whom we read in the New Testament, learned by the study of this poem the duties enjoined by the God of their fathers on those who professed to be his servants. Some of the lessons which it teaches belong especially to older times; to days when patient, unremitting labor, and submission, and modesty, were the virtues most highly commendable in women: but all Scripture has been written for our learning, and its instructions belong to all times; and the Christian woman who has received a larger Bible, and a clearer discovery of divine light, has, while striving to imitate the virtues and graces here enjoined by God's Holy Spirit, the influence of even a stronger motive than any which Jewish females could feel, since Christ has said to his followers, "If ye love me, keep my commandments."

This poem has occupied much of the attention of the learned. The simple reader of Scripture would infer from it one of two things. Either that it was the description of some woman whose character was present to the mind of the writer; or, that it was a picture of such a woman as the inspired writer would propose as a general example. It is by many supposed to have been written by Bathsheba, and intended as a direction to Solomon, under the name of Lemuel, in his choice of a wife.

It would seem, on reading the comments on Scripture, both of old and modern authors, as if learning sometimes served chiefly to perplex and confound simple things. Dr. Doddridge has observed, that the meaning of Scripture, as it presents itself to the unlearned but intelligent reader, is generally the sense in which it is intended; and, though some limitation must be made to this remark, especially in cases in which a knowledge of oriental character and customs aids in so important a manner the illustration of Scripture truth, yet it is, in the main, a just conclusion. Some of the fathers of the church, not content to see in this description a beautiful exhibition of female character, searched for a hidden meaning in its simple declarations. One believed that the virtuous woman shadowed forth the sensitive soul, subject to the understanding and the reason. Another considered that God's holy word, the Scripture of truth, was thus signified. Some thought, with more apparent reason, that it was emblematic of wisdom ; and many, with Ambrose and Bede, have regarded the virtuous woman as a type of the church of Christ. Leaving, however, these mystical and spiritual interpretations of the passage, we shall consider it as an example of moral and religious excellence, presented by God to every woman whose standard of life and character is found in his written word.

The word translated "virtuous," in the first verse of this poem, has a reference also to strength of character, and implies mental and moral energy, or courage. So, too, in the command of the apostle Paul, "Add to your faith virtue," the more strict reading of the word would be, "courage." "The word," says Bishop Patrick, "signifies both strength, or rather courage, and riches, and virtue. Thus, in the description of fitting persons for the magistracy, Jethro, in general, says, they should be *anschee chajil*, which we translate, *able men ;* and then follows more particularly wherein their ability should consist. Such as fear God, men of truth, men hating covetousness. I take therefore the word to include a great fear of God, which is so powerful as to endue one with courage to do well, when piety is contemned, nay,—laughed at and abused."

There is throughout this portrait a firmness and consistency of character, which renders it truly worthy of admiration, and which, owing to the sensibility with which women generally are endued, is a virtue demanding great moral and religious principle. Women, influenced as they necessarily are by their feelings and affections, and rendered, by their dependence on the stronger sex, more liable to adopt the sentiments of others, and to have the character moulded by those to whom they are attached, are peculiarly liable to a want of firmness in conduct. Yet the highest commendation of God is given to this strength of character. We find it recommended in the sacred writings, and especially enjoined on every Christian. "Wherefore add to your faith virtue," says St. Paul; "be ye steadfast, unmovable, always abounding in the work of the Lord." Our Christian profession requires, indeed, to be held with firmness, in days when those who are called Christian women are often found conforming so much to the spirit and manners of the world. "Hold fast," says the apostle, "the confidence and the rejoicing of the hope firm unto the end;" and we are to "hold fast our profession," seeing that we have "a great High Priest, that is passed into the heavens," and therefore by him we may approach boldly unto the throne of grace, to ask for that firmness and consistency which we so much need. And great encouragement, too, is given to firmness; for when we are desired to "hold fast the profession of our faith, without wavering," we are directed to the cheering consideration of the unchanging promises of Christ, "For he is faithful that promised."

There was among the Hebrews a strong and deep earnestness of character, contrasting remarkably with the listlessness and supineness of many oriental people; and the Scripture exhibits numerous instances of moral strength among the Jewish women. There was Miriam, the sister of Moses and Aaron, who, in those days when Israel's God had led them through the dry land, and overwhelmed their enemies in the deep waters, left the privacy of domestic life, and joined with all the Hebrew women in publicly praising their Great Deliverer; and, in a noble fervor of inspired feeling, sang that song, which no poet of later ages has ever equalled in sublimity:

> "Sing ye to the Lord, for he hath triumphed gloriously;
> The horse and his rider hath he thrown into the sea."

There was Deborah, who sat beneath the palm-tree, judging Israel, and even went up fearlessly to the battles of the Lord. There was the noble-minded daughter of the rash Jephthah, whose moral courage failed not in the hour of danger, but who, even in the prospect of personal sacrifices, could rejoice that her father had conquered the enemies of her people; and, with firm integrity, could urge him to keep a promise very injurious to herself. "My father, if thou hast opened thy mouth unto the Lord, do to me according to that which hath proceeded out of thy mouth; forasmuch as the Lord hath taken vengeance for thee of thine enemies, even of the children of Ammon."

In the less troublous times of Israel, no doubt, Jewish women could be found who, like the female of the text, were quietly performing the duties of life, with strength and steadiness of character. But the records of domestic life are written chiefly in the hearts of the home circle; its events, important as they are, not only to that circle, but also, in their eventual influence, on the whole character of a nation, are yet too uniform and simple for the page of either inspired or profane history; and the detail given of the Excellent Woman in this book is the fullest picture which is to be found in the sacred writings of the excellency and employments of a holy woman in her home. Happy is that woman who well performs the duties of home, to whom home is the sphere which concentrates her ambition, and has the largest share of her love; and who governs her household actively and diligently, and in the fear of the Lord.

But, although no other part of Scripture gives so connected a detail of a pious woman's works and duties, yet all the various directions to the female sex, with which the writings of the apostles abound, accord with its principles. "Wives, submit yourselves unto your own husbands, as it is fit in the Lord;" even so must the wives "be grave, not slanderers, sober, faithful in all things."

Again: she is to be well reported of for good works; if she have brought up children, if she have lodged strangers, if she have washed the saints' feet, if she have relieved the afflicted, if she have diligently followed every good work. "In behavior," good wives were to be "as becometh holiness: not false accusers, not given to much wine, teachers of good things;—to be sober, to love their husbands, to love their children. To be discreet, chaste, keepers at home."

It was from such holy mothers that the saints of the New Testament were descended. Of such a mother and such a grandmother, young Timothy learned the Holy Scriptures. In homes like this were reared Martha and Mary, those sisters of Bethany, that family whom Jesus loved, and one of whom he gently reproved, because her energy of character led her to a restless anxiety of serving at a moment when she should have sat and listened to the words of her Lord. In households like these dwelt the mother of our Saviour, and Elizabeth, the blessed of the Lord,—names ever dear to us all. From such sprung Priscilla, who received the young Apollos into her home, and expounded unto him the way of God more perfectly; and who, with her husband, is said by the apostle to have been ready, for his life, to have laid down their own necks. Of such were Phebe, the servant of the church at Cenchrea; and Mary, who bestowed much labor on the ministers of Christ; and many others, who, when faithful steadfastness and pious strength of resolution led to death, yet shrunk not even from suffering, but joined the noble army of martyrs, and are among those who "came out of great tribulation, and have washed their robes, and made them white in the blood of the Lamb."

Even in that deeply solemn hour when the blessed Saviour yielded his life on the cross, to atone for sinful man,—at an hour when the fear of death had power to triumph over the faith of many,—when his disciples forsook him and fled,—yet holy women shrunk not from following him to the cross.

When foes the hand of menace shook,
And friends betrayed, denied, forsook,
Then woman, meekly constant still,
Followed to Calvary's fatal hill:
    Yes, followed where the boldest failed,
      Unmoved by threat or sneer:

For faithful woman's love prevailed
O er helpless woman's fear.

To a woman, the pious virgin Mary, the mother of the Saviour, his dying eyes were directed, and his dying bequest made, that the beloved disciple would take her to his own home. O that woman's steadfastness of character may shrink not, either in the day of persecution or in the daily acts of household duty, since strength and wisdom are given now by him who gave it to holy women of old; that now, as then, they may follow the Lord fully! The example here given should lead every female to seek from the Holy Spirit the grace to abound in holy courage and devotedness to the Lord.

Woman! blest partner of our joys and woes!
Even in the darkest hour of earthly ill,
Untarnished yet thy fond affection glows,
Throbs with each pulse, and beats with every thrill!
When sorrow rends the heart, when feverish pain
Wrings the hot drops of anguish from the brow, —
To soothe the soul, to cool the burning brain,
O! who so welcome and so prompt as thou?

SECTION II.

THE HEART OF HER HUSBAND DOTH SAFELY TRUST IN HER, SO THAT HE SHALL HAVE NO NEED OF SPOIL.

Confidence of such a kind implies not only a conviction of simplicity and guilelessness of character in the wife, but it also assures us of her discretion. No man could safely trust in one whose conduct was not unspotted in all her intercourse with society. The heart of her husband had no care, lest, by any unguarded act, any imprudence on her part, she should bring a reproach upon his name, or a sorrow into his bosom. Such a woman must have shunned even the appearance of evil. She must have acted on the principle of the Hebrew proverb, "A good name is better than precious ointment, and loving favor to be chosen rather than choice gold;" and, by the uniform consistency of a virtuous life, have gained the entire confidence of him who best knew her character.

The
HEART OF HER HUSBAND
DOTH SAFELY TRUST IN HER,
SO THAT HE SHALL HAVE
NO NEED OF SPOIL.

But while the text implies this, yet it mainly refers to the assurance entertained by her husband of her care and skill in the management of her household. Archbishop Cranmer renders this passage, "So that he shall fall into no poverty," and Boothroyd translates it, "And of his property he will not be deprived." The Septuagint version understands the word spoil as referring to the woman, and not to her husband; "Such an one as she shall not want good spoils." But in any case it signifies that provident care and management, that looking after the concerns of her family, for which we find her so often commended throughout the poem.

The need of spoil must be explained by a reference to the usages of the Hebrews at this period of society. The Israelites had often obtained spoils in their encounters with neighboring nations. The reign of David had been occupied by continual warfare. The pastoral community at this time were not a tribe of idle shepherds, but those who had been men of war from their youth; and their frequent expeditions were regarded as acts of retaliation for similar offences from the herdsmen of neighboring tribes. Saul and David had been great warriors; and under the latter king, the Israelites had been so trained to military discipline that they appear to have been always victorious in the field, and are frequently represented as sharing that spoil which in the more peaceful days of Solomon was less generally enjoyed. The first public act of Saul had been a battle against Nahash the Ammonite; and in the description of the spoil taken, when Saul and Jonathan, and all the Hebrews, encountered the Philistines, we see the nature of the wealth gained by the Israelites. In the narrative given in 1 Samuel xv., we find that the people flew upon the spoil, and took sheep and oxen and calves. And when, in the following chapter, we read that Saul fought against the Amalekites, and sinned against Jehovah by appropriating, as spoil, those things which he had commanded him to destroy, we find enumerated the sheep and oxen and lambs, which formed the wealth of a pastoral people.

But if Saul, as had been sung by the Hebrew maidens, had slain his thousands, David had slain his tens of thousands, and the records of his life display how much wealth had been gained by the Israelites from their enemies. At the time when David, driven from his home by the jealousy of

Saul, wandered with his men to the wilderness of Paran, they probably supported themselves by spoil gathered from the tribes who came down upon the shepherds of the land. The narrative of Nabal's churlishness refers to David's protection of the herdsmen from incursions of this nature; for when their unthankful master refused his help to the wanderer, the young men told Abigail, and said of David's host, "They were a wall unto us both by night and day, all the while we were with them keeping sheep." And now, when peace was in Israel generally, yet in adjacent countries the same practices were continued, and the man who sought to be rich often shared the spoil taken from others.

But in the case of this Jewish family there was no need of such spoil. Industry supplied the household wants, and care kept that from waste which industry had gathered, and the husband had no occasion to go out to warfare. Under the shadow of his own vine and his own fig-tree he could enjoy the blessings of a peaceful life; and in his earthly home could find that love and quietness which might prove the best foretaste that earth can give of the heavenly home to which he was tending.

SECTION III.

SHE WILL DO HIM GOOD, AND NOT EVIL, ALL THE DAYS OF HER LIFE.

Under every circumstance of life, it is in the power of those who dwell in the same household to benefit each other. Hourly opportunities occur of showing kindness, of practising forbearance, and of constantly doing good. But this is most especially the case with husbands and wives. If we except the strongest of all earthly influences,—that of the mother on her child,—there is none which can equal that of the conjugal relation. Time and eternity are connected with it. Happiness or misery is dependent on the way in which it is exercised; so important is it, that the wise and inspired man said, "A good wife is from the Lord."

"See that ye love one another with a pure heart fervently," said the apostle Peter, enjoining on the early converts the duties of the Christian life; and if this is commanded to all, how much

She

WILL DO HIM GOOD,

AND NOT EVIL, ALL THE

DAYS OF HER LIFE.

more is it to be cultivated by those who are attached by the strongest domestic tie! And as no marriage should be contracted without mutual love, so the principle of love should guide a woman in all her married life, and lead her always to do good to her husband.

A wife can do much good to her husband by promoting his domestic comfort. This is, indeed, placed almost wholly in her hands; it rests with her to see that the fireside is the place of attraction, that home is the brightest spot on earth. And love will teach ingenuity to the faithful wife, and show to her a thousand ways by which she may endear the home circle. If she wish to enjoy her husband's society, she must be a keeper at home; and so arrange her family as that he, when he returns from the care and noise and contention of the world, shall find a retreat in which sweet converse shall beguile him of his cares, and peace, and love, and order, and gentle welcome, and soothing sympathy, shall form a striking contrast to the scenes he has just quitted.

Another way in which we may feel certain that the matron of the text did good to her husband, was by sharing his cares. On many, in modern times, the charge is not incumbent of laboring with the hands to provide food and raiment for the family, as did this eminent example of female virtue. The different constitution of modern society has placed upon men the duty of maintaining a family, and left to woman the sweeter privilege of ordering the charities of home. Yet, even now, a wife may do much to lessen the cares of a husband. She may not fully understand the nature of his employments, she cannot exactly enter into the details of his business; but she can give the attentive ear; she can endeavor to comprehend his difficulties; she can forbear the mention of any irritating domestic circumstances; she can soften down annoyances. Sometimes she can cheer him by reminding him of some consoling promise of God's word. She can show him the command of holy writ, to cast his care upon God. She can tell him that "they that seek the Lord shall not want any good thing," and perhaps lead him to say, with David, "What time I am afraid, I will trust in thee." And when all these fail, and her anxious eye sees the cloud still darken over his brow, then she can pray, with a firm, unwavering faith, that God would indeed "lift up the light of his countenance upon him, and give him peace."

Nor is it less her duty to share in his joys. If her husband have succeeded in some pursuit, with what heartiness should the wife enter into his pleasure! Never should the wandering eye betray that she listens with indifference to the details which interest him. She should value his pursuits, if for no other reason than because they are his; and by an ever ready sympathy should "do him good, and not evil," all the days of her life. Never should the depressing fear or the ardent hope be thrown coldly back again on him who utters it. One such repulsion will do more to alienate the love of a sensitive mind than many little acts of neglect or annoyance.

A wife will also do her husband good by encouraging him to holiness and virtue, and warning him against sin. In the intimacy of domestic life, the first tendency to evil is sometimes evident to the wife, and it is her duty to rebuke with all gentleness, and to plead with all earnestness, against conduct which may be displeasing to God and man.

Abigail's reproof and counsel of David is a beautiful instance of womanly tact and delicacy thus employed. When Nabal, in return for David's kindness and protection, had contemptuously refused refreshments to the warrior shepherd, how does Abigail propitiate David's wrath, and dissuade him from revenge! "And it shall come to pass, when the Lord shall have done to my lord according to all the good that he hath spoken concerning thee, and shall have appointed thee ruler over Israel; that this shall be no grief unto thee, nor offence of heart unto my lord, either that thou hast shed blood causeless, or that my lord hath avenged himself." And, in like manner, how often may the wife expostulate with her husband, and thus keep him from evil that it may not grieve him; and in after days he may look back with gratitude and affection for the warning voice which checked his onward course, and bade him pause and consider.

The wife of the text did her husband no evil. She neither wasted his wealth nor neglected his comfort, nor was careless of his reputation, nor provoked him to anger. She loved him with a steady love, all the days of her life; in joy and in sorrow, in sickness and in health. Years passed on, and saw it fixed, while all around was changing. It was not like the vapory cloud upon the blue sky, driven about by every wind of heaven, and skimming lightly over the surface; but as the rock in the midst of the waters, against which the waves might dash and bring no change, and on which all the alternations of sun and wind fell harmlessly, and which stood unshaken by all things. Seldom is love like this,—love which can bear the test of time and the shock of adversity,—love which can flourish even amid infirmities; seldom is it found but in the home of the loved and loving.

They who love us till we die,
  Who in sorrow have been tried,
Who will watch our closing eye,
  When all grows cold beside:
Where shall friends like these be found,
  Search the earth and ocean wide;
On what hallowed spot of ground,
  Save our own fireside?

SECTION IV.

SHE SEEKETH WOOL AND FLAX, AND WORKETH WILLINGLY WITH HER HANDS.

Obviously the whole description given by the inspired writer of the employments of the Jewish matron belongs either to primitive ages, or to those pastoral regions of modern times, in which commerce with other nations has made little progress, and foreign manufactures are almost unknown. Recently, the Hebrew people had been engaged continually in battle, and now the men of Israel were chiefly occupied with agriculture and pastoral employments. Trade with other lands was confined to occasional barter, and the various stuffs requisite for the clothing of the household, though sometimes wrought by the professed weaver, were chiefly fabricated by the hands of the mistresses or maidens of the Jewish homes. Solomon, indeed, had fetched spices from Arabia, and fine linen from Egypt; and, in his love for

She

SEEKETH WOOL AND FLAX, AND WORKETH WILLINGLY WITH HER HANDS.

natural history, had assembled in his capital the birds and animals of distant countries; yet his traffic seems to have been almost confined to his own requirements, and not to have extended itself to his subjects. In such a state of society, the domestic industry of the female part of the population becomes so necessary, that it is always encouraged and valued. The ancient Romans, under circumstances somewhat similar, expected from their wives a great degree of attention to household employments, and this was enjoined by their marriage rites. So also among the Greeks, in the early ages of the world, the mistress worked with her servants, and the high-born lady, as well as the daughter of the peasant, performed those humble and more active duties generally left, in our time and country, to the poor. Homer intimates that the daughters of princes washed, in the fountain, the clothing of the family; while from Scripture we learn that Rebecca, the heiress of a pastoral prince, gave drink to the servant of Abraham, and afterwards drew water for himself and his cattle. Rachel, too, the beautiful daughter of one who possessed sheep and herds in abundance, yet kept her father's flocks on the plains of Syria, exposed to the scorching heat of day, if not to the heavy dews of night. Even now, in the pastoral regions of Asia, it is the glory of a woman that her own hand has wrought the clothing of her husband, son, or brother, and has decked the walls of their dwellings; and a helpless, useless woman would be despised by the other females of her tribe.

So it was of old,
That woman's hand, amid the elements
Of patient industry and household good,
Reproachless wrought, twining the slender thread
From the light distaff; or in skilful loom
Weaving rich tissues, or with glowing tints
Of rich embroidery, pleased to decorate
The mantle of her lord. And it was well;
For in such sheltered and congenial sphere
Content with duty dwells.

And this diligent industry, so applicable to the wants of the people, had its praise of God, while the luxurious and delicate habits of the daughters of Zion, in later ages, are marked with his displeasure. It is with stern reprobation that the prophet Isaiah speaks of the rings, and chains, and mufflers, and fine linen, of the Jewish ladies, whose haughty demeanor called for the solemn threatenings of God; and all whose ornaments were to be forgotten soon, when Zion, the faithless Zion, should be full of mourning and lamentation, and, "being desolate, should sit upon the ground."

Owing to the almost unchanging customs of Eastern nations, the people of modern Palestine are probably clothed nearly in the same manner as the ancient Hebrews, and a variety of woollen and linen garments are still worn in that land. When Hannah made the young Samuel a little coat, and brought it to him, year by year, as she came up with her husband to the yearly sacrifice, she performed the part of a mother in Israel; and, in all likelihood, carried to her beloved child a garment of pure white linen, or wool, for such were much worn by the ancient Jews, to whom frequent purifications and washings were commanded by Israel's God. It might have been, however, a coat, like that of Joseph, of many colors, for brilliant dyes and skilful embroidery were often used by the Israelites to ornament their dresses. One prohibition on the subject of woollen clothing had been given to the Jews. God had forbidden them to wear a garment made of woollen and linen, for in such a dress the heathen priests worshipped their false gods, in the superstitious hope of a blessing on their flax and their sheep; and the one true God, the great Jehovah, would that his chosen race should come out from idolaters, and be a separate people.

The excellent woman whom we are considering was evidently a person of wealth and distinction, she was the wife of one who sat among the elders of the land, and we may reasonably suppose that she gathered the flax from her own fields, as well as that the wool was the produce of her own flocks. Flax was one of the plants earliest cultivated by mankind in masses. Its bright green stalks withered before the plague of hail which came upon Egypt, when the flax and barley were smitten; and its bright blue flower seems to have been very abundant in

> That fertile land, where mighty Moses stretched
> His rod miraculous.

A little later in the history of the world we find a woman preparing it for use; for Rahab had laid the stalks of flax on the roof of her house, that the scorching sun and the damp Syrian dews might macerate its fibres, when the spies entreated her compassion, and were hidden by her among the half-dried plants. "By comparing the several passages in Scripture," says Kitto, "in which flax is mentioned, we shall find the amount to be, that flax was cultivated to a considerable extent in Palestine; that garments of it were worn not only by the priests and Levites, but very largely by the people. The coarse linen cloths were manufactured at home by the women, but the finer were imported from Egypt; the ancient celebrity of which country, for its linen fabrics, is abundantly confirmed in Scripture. We cannot find that flax is now much cultivated in Palestine, although considerable attention is paid to the culture of cotton. It may be that the soil and climate are less suited than that of Egypt to its production."

There is a cheerfulness and a heartiness in the character which the inspired writer gives of the Jewish woman. She "worketh willingly," or, as some translate it, "with the delight of her hands;" and it is this willingness which lends a grace to every household employment, and infuses a spirit of alacrity into the daily duties of life. Cheerful willingness is no small virtue in a woman; for the duties performed with a smiling countenance and a ready hand are far differently done from those which seem wrung out of necessity, and are accompanied by a mournful voice and a languid footstep. A willing mind is enjoined, by God's word, on every performance of duty. With the Most High, the motive of the heart is regarded, rather than the outward act. So we learn that, in working for God, "if there be first a willing mind, it is accepted according to that a man hath, and not according to that he hath not:" while to both mistress and servant comes the exhortation respecting the humble duties of every-day life, "Whatsoever ye do, do it heartily, as to the Lord, and not unto men."

If we consider the benefits which we hourly receive from the Great Giver of all good gifts, we shall see that a willing cheerfulness is indeed but the proper response which should be given by his human family. There may, it is true, be a cheerfulness which is in no way connected with thankfulness, but never yet was there a thankful spirit which did not lead to acts of cheerful service. And, notwithstanding the various sorrows which sin has brought into the world, yet how much remains to gladden the heart of one who is disposed to observe God's goodness! How do all our senses minister to enjoyment! The sense of touch and the sense of taste are continually gratified, and delicious odors greet us from a thousand flowers. And the eye of man, how is it an inlet to wisdom, and what beautiful forms and what gorgeous colorings please our sight, and thus charm our imagina tion, till we are lost in wonder at the sublime, oı melt in tenderness at lowly beauty! And the ear, too, made as it is to receive the impression of all sweet sounds and concords, how do the tunes of birds, and the roar of waters, and the sweet tink lings of the distant bell, and the low murmuring of the pleasant brooks, and the soothing influence of kindly voices, bring through it a song of joy to the spirit, or, sweeter still, a song of softened and pensive tunefulness. And when outward nature speaks to us through the senses, then and then only is it rightly received, while it tells of God and his goodness and wher the grateful heart prompts words of thankfulness to the ready tongue, and the willing hand performs the active service, in the spirit of him who said, "What shall I render unto the Lord for all his mercies?"

And if all might render willing service to God in acknowledgment of mercies, how much more shall the child of God be ready to perform every duty with an enlightened thankfulness? To him is given the precious Bible; on him are bestowed its promises, cheering him under every sorrow, and telling him that God is with him in the darkest hour, yea, even in the valley of the shadow of death. To him is access given to the throne of grace, so that his prayers rise up to God, through the intercession of the great Mediator. For him the Saviour lived a life of sorrow and humiliation, and died a dishonored death, that his sins might be pardoned, and his soul saved from the wrath which God denounces against the transgressors of his holy law. To him are often given holy aspirations after God's presence, and a sure sense of his love; so that he seems able to join even in the songs of heaven, and his spirit seems carried away for a while from his earthly house up to that glorious home of rest which is eternal, and where God and the blessed angels shall at last receive him.

Every one must have remarked how pleasant is that household in which a cheerful spirit of energy is cultivated by the mistress and mother. It is a pleasant thing to dwell with one who is not troubled by trifling annoyances, who is skilled in looking at the bright side of things, and hoping for the best; with one who believes that all the ways of the Lord are right, and who attaches a deep importance to duty. Such a one will work willingly, in the belief that God has appointed both her lot and her duties; and it is surprising how many obstacles are met and overcome by such a spirit.

> The wise and active conquer difficulties
> By daring to attempt them. Sloth and folly
> Shiver and shrink at sight of toil and trouble,
> And make the impossibilities they fear.

The employments of daily life, of women especially, need often the remembrance that they are done in the sight of him in whose eye the lowliest act is of importance. There are many persons who do not perform them well, because they do not look upon them as part of their religious duties. Such persons could perhaps make great sacrifices for conscience' sake; they could act nobly and wisely if any great service were demanded; but they do not consider that the whole progress of human life consists of a succession of small acts. It is often with smaller duties as with smaller trials, that strength to do or to bear is not sought of God. Some great trial befalls us, some important sacrifice is required, and, feeling our helplessness, we fall back upon God, and support is given; but every-day events are, by their very monotony, unimpressive; we think lightly of them, and the help of God is not sought, and they are not duly considered, and so are performed in a careless, perhaps in an unwilling spirit. But he who is the Judge of all the earth looks down with approval on the mother whose life is one daily course of self-sacrifice, on the daughter whose gentle smiles and willing work render home happy, rather than on her who is roused from a course of usual listlessness to some one act of great exertion, or to some one costly deed of self-denial. The flash of lightning produces a great effect; and the clearer air and the cloudless sky show that it has well performed God's mission; yet who would not rather that her light should shine like that of the evening star, whose tranquil rays nightly guide the traveller home, and cheer the mariner on the deep, and smile sweetly on the shepherd who watches by his fold, till they "fade away into the light of heaven"?

> Who's born for sloth? To some we find
> The ploughshare's annual toil assigned;
> Some at the sounding anvil glow;
> Some the swift-sliding shuttle throw;
> Some, studious of the wind and tide,
> From pole to pole our commerce guide;
> While some, of genius more refined,
> With head and tongue assist mankind.
> In every rank, or great or small,
> 'T is industry supports us all.

SECTION V.

SHE IS LIKE THE MERCHANTS' SHIPS; SHE BRINGETH HER FOOD FROM AFAR.

Merchants' ships, in King Solomon's days, might, indeed, be said to bring their cargoes from afar. If we look at the record of the sea voyages made at that time, when the Hebrew King was assisted by Hiram, who furnished him with "shipmen who had knowledge of the sea," we shall find that they occupied a very considerable period. "For the king had at sea a navy of Tarshish with the navy of Hiram; once in three years came the navy of Tarshish, bringing gold, and silver, ivory, and apes, and peacocks." The Phœnicians, who resided on the north-west of Palestine, are known to have had a commercial settlement, called Tartessus, on the Atlantic coast of Spain, near the modern Cadiz; and, whatever may be the various opinions respecting the location of ancient Ophir, there is little doubt that this port was the

She
IS LIKE
THE MERCHANTS' SHIPS;
SHE BRINGETH
HER FOOD
FROM AFAR.

Tarshish of the Scriptures. In the imperfect state of navigation, the voyages, performed as they were in small and ill-constructed vessels, would seem to the Israelites "afar," indeed, and attended with very considerable peril.

But, as food rather than other merchandise seems alluded to in the text, it is probable that the ships which brought corn from Egypt are here referred to. Although the ancient Hebrews were decidedly an agricultural community, and the rich valley of Palestine abounded in corn and wine, yet, in seasons of dearth, as well as on other occasions, the Jewish people appear to have traded with Egypt for corn. On the fertile lands of that well-watered country corn grew so abundantly that Egypt was the general granary of the East; and the touching narrative of Joseph and his brethren at once occurs to the mind, as an instance in which men went down into Egypt to buy corn.

The Israelites were by no means a maritime people; yet bordered as the Holy Land was by the Great Sea, now called the Mediterranean, which was the very highway of commerce, and familiar as they were with the Nile, on whose shores their fathers had rendered a hard service to the line of Pharaohs, they doubtless had many ships of burden, which were, at least, as well constructed as those in the western parts of the world at the same period of time. It must be remembered that their vessels were almost exclusively ships of merchandise. As yet, no battle-ship had carried proud defiance to the peaceful shores; no cannon thundered its awful challenges on the deep; but the ship, in its occasional course over the waters, brought from afar the luxuries or the food of other lands, and bore in its welcome progress nothing to fill the heart with sorrow, or to leave a trace of that anguish and desolation which war brings so often now over the distant sea.

Very early mention is made in Scripture of ships. "Zebulun shall dwell at the haven of the sea; and he shall be for an haven of ships," was the prophecy of the dying patriarch, as his eye, though dimmed to the sights of this world by the film of death, glanced forth and kindled at the view of futurity; and yet no regular trade by sea seems to have been established in Solomon's day, since he was obliged to seek aid from Hiram Many beau tiful spots on the shores of the sea are familiar to Scripture readers, and the vessels which floated on the Lake of Gennesareth were often honored by the presence of Him who disdained not the poor and the lowly, but gathered his apostles from among fishermen, and, standing on the brow of a Jewish vessel, delivered to the people on the shore those beautiful parables, and those teachings of heavenly love and wisdom, which brought many to his feet as his disciples, and are now the treasure of millions of hearts, to whom the truths taught by the Saviour are dearer than gold or silver, more precious than life itself.

The Jewish matron, whose various kinds of manufacture are so specifically named, would have much to offer in exchange either for corn or other commodities, which the merchants' ships convey. Garments made of fine wool or of hair stuffs, gorgeous tapestry wrought by her own hands, fine linen girdles,—all were suitable objects of barter; and the rich clusters of grapes which her vineyard could furnish, and the well-dried flax from her fields, constituted a store from which something might be well spared. It seems probable, however, that the articles chiefly sent by her, either to distant tribes, or perhaps occasionally to lands beyond the seas, were those costly and magnificent dresses which form the wealth of the eastern female, and which are highly scented with perfumes, and laid up for many years, to be brought out only on important occasions. The use of dresses also as presents, in the East, would render the barter of them a very likely and considerable source of profit; and this would enable this Jewish lady, whose intelligent and well-devoted industry is so often commended, to procure for her family some of those enjoyments from afar, which the home produce would not supply.

Let us, then, be up and doing,
With a heart for any fate;
Still achieving, still pursuing,
Learn to labor and to wait.

She riseth also while it is
yet night, and giveth
meat to her
household, and a
portion to her maidens.

SECTION VI.

SHE RISETH ALSO WHILE IT IS YET NIGHT, AND GIVETH MEAT TO HER HOUSEHOLD, AND A PORTION TO HER MAIDENS.

A Proverb in the preceding part of this book says that "every wise woman buildeth her house, while the foolish plucketh it down with her hands." The stability and comfort of the household are, indeed, so dependent on the domestic arrangements of her who presides,—punctuality and order in the wife are so necessary for the preservation of the property which may have been acquired,—that the truth of the old Irish saying, "A man must ask his wife's leave to be rich," is very apparent. Early risers will not often be found among those whose habits are irregular and disorderly. The practice of beginning the work with the commencement of the day is almost always found in conjunction with punctual and diligent habits, and with the love of order and management as described in the text.

The learned Aben Ezra poetically interprets the expression of the former part of the verse, "She riseth before the ascent of day." Early rising in the East is different from that of our native land. To be up with the lark, or when the robin is first uttering his morning song,—to brush away the pearls from the grass, while the sun is just driving afar the gray mists of the morning,—this is, with us, to rise early. But the diligent man of eastern lands is up long before sunrise, long before

> "Morn, her rosy steps
> Advancing, sows the earth with orient pearls;"

and has begun his labor at an hour when the European is sleeping still, with the sound sleep of midnight. And when the dawn breaks over the vineyards of Palestine, and the sun sheds his red lustre on her ruddy hills, the vine-dresser has tended his vine, and the shepherd has led forth his flock from the fold. In the city, too, the merchant is busy in the shop; and the courtier and the king are occupied in the business of the court; and the women are spinning the web of industry. Among the Hebrews, it was also customary for the diligent women to be up earlier than the men; for adding to the usual domestic employments of females in general the duty of manufacturing various fabrics of use or merchandise, the day was never too long for their busy skill, and they knew nothing of that weariness which belongs to the idle, and which deprives them of that freshness and energy of character which make existence a blessing.

We find continual reference in Scripture to the habit of beginning the business of the day at a very early hour in the morning. Thus, when Moses was sent to Pharaoh, by the Lord God of the Hebrews, and the haughty king was commanded to let the people of Israel go out from their cruel bondage, the Jewish lawgiver was commanded to rise up early in the morning, and to stand before Pharaoh as "he cometh forth to the water." And when the vain and deceitful Absalom sought to win away the hearts of Israel from their allegiance to his father, "he rose up early, and stood beside the way of the gate" of the city; for he well knew, that, passing through its arches, he should meet those who were going out of the town to the daily labor of the fields, or find there assembled the concourse of merchants. And in that day of Israel's affliction and reproach, when the walls of Jerusalem had been broken down, and the gates thereof burned with fire, and Nehemiah and the Jews labored amidst danger and anxiety to build again the walls of their beloved city, we find them early at their work, cheered by the promises and prayers of the diligent prophet; and while some labored, half of them "held the spears from the rising of the morning till the stars appeared." And well would it be for us if we could return to the early rising and retiring, once general even in our own land, when our forefathers saw the sun set on their native hills, and slept on their less luxurious couches, at an hour far earlier than the business of the day now closes on busy multitudes.

The description given by the Hebrew writer is so graphic, that our imaginations can easily picture the Jewish matron, as surrounded by her family at early day, and apportioning to each of her household, not only daily food, but also daily work. One is going to the field; another, to relieve the herdsman who has watched through the starry night on the hill-side, or on the plain. Her daughters and her maidens will ply the distaff, or with the needle weave delicate embroideries; and the materials for the work of each must be selected, and, by a judicious division of labor, all be made easy. And in this diligent and well-ordered family, not only must the domestic animals be cared for, but the young infant must be tended, and the older child taught to walk in wisdom's ways, and to know the law of the God of Israel. The word here translated "portion" seems certainly to include work as well as food. The Targum renders it by service, and interprets the passage as meaning employment, rather than a portion of daily meat. The same word is used in Exodus 5: 14, when the task-masters of the children of Israel demanded, "Wherefore have ye not fulfilled your *task* in making brick both yesterday and to-day as heretofore?" The Septuagint, as well as the Syriac and Arabic versions, render the word "works."

The ancient custom of dividing the food into separate portions is alluded to not only in several parts of the Sacred Scripture, but is frequently mentioned by profane writers. Thus, when the ambassadors of Agamemnon were received at the table of Achilles, the warrior distributed to every man his portion. Among the Romans an officer presided over this distribution at the ancient meal, and seems to have borne a similar office to him who is mentioned, in the narrative of the marriage of Cana, as the governor of the feast. And when Joseph entertained his brethren who had come up to Egypt, we mark how, with the peculiar love which the man of the East feels for the brother who claims the same mother as himself, he apportioned to his beloved Benjamin a mess five times as large as that of any of his other brethren. Not but that each had a portion large enough for his refreshment, but that a stronger warmth of hospitality might mark his deeper love to him whom his dying mother had called "the son of my sorrow."

The right economy of time is a highly important duty. To those who are called to exercise the duties of active life, this is very evident. The mistress, the mother, and the domestic servant, these will all feel the value of time; yet no gift is more often wasted by those to whom God has allotted a large portion of leisure. The waste of time is a sin especially chargeable on a large number of the female sex in the present day. Hours are wasted in frivolous accomplishments; in the performance of some of the lighter works of art; in dissipated visiting; in reading novels and idle books, and in absolute lounging and indolence; so that if we could trace the history of the life of many an English woman, we should find her employments of little more worth to herself and others than those of the butterfly which skims from flower to flower, the gay creature of the summer's day. And yet to every reasonable being existence brings an amount of responsibility which we shall comprehend only in eternity. Time is given us for duty, for the preparation for a future state, for the good of others; and every fragment of it should be gathered up, that nothing of so precious a gift may be lost. It should become a subject of deep and frequent thought to every woman, and especially to every Christian woman, whether her time is rightly spent. Owing to the great improvements in manufactures, and the high civilization of modern society, women in the middle and higher classes of life are rarely required to apply unremittingly to any pursuit which can be called toil or labor. Many have no pursuit at all. And is there nothing to do, that God should look down on the couch of the luxurious, when the morning sun has long shed his light on its drapery, and should see the sleeper still seeking repose? Is there nothing that the daughter or sister can do to lighten the cares or anxieties of parents or brothers? Is there no active duty, which, if cheerfully done, would make home happier? If we are not required, like the excellent women of old, to rise while it is yet night, and to apportion to those of our household food or work, yet there is still enough to do. There are our hearts to examine, as in the sight of God. There are prayer and meditation, and reading of the Scripture, all best done in the quiet of early day, ere the noise and tumult of the tempting world have distracted the thoughts. David could say, when referring to his moments of prayer, "My soul prevented the dawning of the morning," and could deem it a "good thing" to "show forth the loving kindness of the Lord in the morning;" and as his soul thirsted for God, he exclaimed, "Early will I seek thee." In the solemn moment of approaching suffering, our Saviour himself rose a great while before day, that he might commune with his Father.

But, beside the study of God's word, there is also the duty of mental improvement. For this end, we should seek to redeem the time, and see that the early hours are not wasted. An hour gained daily from sleep,—how much might be done with this, in the study of any valuable species of knowledge! How much might we learn of any one portion of nature, by an hour of daily reading and observation! And does not nature tell of God? It is not the stars alone, and the sun and moon, which speak of God's greatness and power, and so from day unto day utter speech, and from night unto night teach knowledge. All his works praise him. The sea, with its ebb and flow, and changing tides, and all its curious store of weeds and corals, and its silver-spangled fishes, has a wondrous lesson to teach the docile spirit, of God's power and love. The softly-flowing stream, gladdening the verdant herbage, and serving as a home of happiness to the living creatures which inhabit it, and as a scene of sport to the brilliant-winged insects, of all the bright hues of earth and heaven, which hover above it; the flowery meadow and the dark-robed forest; the bird, with its plumage dipped in hues of Paradise, and its song suggesting thoughts of poetry, — all, all have been studied by human minds, which have lived in ages before we were born, and their wonders and their histories have been traced by human pens, and we may read their records in books, and learn their teachings beneath the morning sunshine. And health, too, that valuable blessing, how greatly is it promoted by early hours! Many diseases, and especially those called nervous disorders, were almost unknown in Britain a few ages since, when luxury had not yet made it a common practice to be found in bed in full day. Many serious illnesses would take their flight before the long-continued and diligent practice of an early morning walk; and the cheek now pale from indolent habits, and the eye now dim from want of the exercise required by the frame, might glow and sparkle with the bloom and vigor of life, if, like the country laborer or the diligent rustic maiden, and the excellent woman of the text, we should rise with the ascent of day. And if we redeemed an hour in the morning, it might leave us one in the after day to visit the poor and afflicted, to instruct the ignorant, to help those who need our aid. If household duties demanded exertion, then the gained hour might enable us to pass through them more leisurely and more pleasantly, and we might be saved the irritation of hurried business; or, if we gave that hour to God, who shall say what blessings our prayers might bring down on ourselves and on those dear to us, on the church of God and on the world at large!

Her might is gentleness; she winneth sway
By a soft word and softer look;
Where she, the gentle, loving one, hath failed,
The proud or stern might never yet succeed.

Strength, power and majesty, belong to man;
They make the glory native to his life;
But sweetness is a woman's attribute;
By that she reigns, and will forever reign.

There have been some who, with a mightier mind,
Have won dominion; but they never won
The dearer empire of the beautiful,—
Sweet sovereigns of their natural loveliness.

SECTION VII.

SHE CONSIDERETH A FIELD, AND BUYETH IT: WITH THE FRUIT OF HER HANDS SHE PLANTETH A VINEYARD.

While we observe how various were the employments of the Hebrew woman, we cannot fail to remark the great and entire confidence which must have been placed in her by her husband. That he should leave to her care the management of her house and servants, and in great measure the training of her children, seems, at all times, natural, and in the state of society we are considering, peculiarly so; but we should scarcely expect to find a Jewish female left so entirely to her own judgment in matters of business. It was probably, however, not unusual at this time. Abigail, the wife of Nabal, it seems, had entire command over the family property, when she took two hundred loaves, and two bottles of wine, and five sheep ready dressed, and fruits, and other valuable articles of food, and gave

SHE CONSIDERETH A FIELD, AND BUYETH IT; WITH THE FRUIT OF HER HANDS SHE PLANTETH A VINEYARD.

them to David. That the woman of the text was worthy of this entire confidence is very evident, for hers was the systematic industry of a well-ordered mind, and not the occasional result of mere impulse. She deliberated on the best plan to be pursued. She saw that her children were rising up, her household numerous, her husband a man of wealth and distinction; and the requirements of such a family demanded a careful consideration.

Perhaps, in looking around her in order to make a provision for an increasing household, the eye of the Hebrew woman often rested on some field of waving corn which lay near her own estate; and she saw, in its golden ears, the prospect of an abundant store for the food of her family; and then, with the fruits of her own hands, the works which her own fingers had wrought, she purchased the land. The luxuriant vegetation of the vineyard, watered by the fruitful rill, or lying on the hill-side, where the morning sun shed most of his light and warmth, would attract her notice, and the wild roses, and the bright pomegranates, shedding the deep red lustre of their flowers in the hedges which surrounded it, and wafting to her some of the sweetest of eastern odors, would convince her that the soil which yielded them would repay careful culture.

The rich drapery of the vine, though now less cultivated in the Holy Land, once formed one of its most striking and picturesque objects. Far away over the hills of the then fruitful, though now neglected Palestine, might be heard the joyous song of the vine-dressers, speaking of peace and plenty, and attesting the happy feeling and the joyous emotion of the natives of a pure and lovely climate, whose animal spirits and earnest feelings seemed wrought upon by the gladness of nature, till they flowed forth in song. And many a pious Israelite may have sung with the sweet singer of his country, "The earth is the Lord's, and the fulness thereof;" and as he looked upon his rich corn-fields, have chanted gladly, "Thou visitest the earth, and waterest it; thou greatly enrichest it with the river of God, which is full of water; thou preparest them corn, when thou hast so provided for it. Thou crownest the year with thy goodness; and thy paths drop fatness."

But although the modern inhabitant of Palestine

no longer labors assiduously, as did the ancient Israelite, to render his beautiful land an earthly paradise, though in many parts joy and gladness have ceased from the fruitful field, and all the daughters of music are brought low, yet the vineyards are often beautiful still. On the Syrian hills and plains may yet be seen the tower or the lonely cottage in a vineyard, on which the eye of the evangelical prophet rested when he foretold the desolation of the daughter of Zion; or when he spake of the vineyard in the fruitful hill, planted with the choicest vine, in which the lord of the vineyard built a tower, and made a wine-press, and looked for the grateful fruits of his culture, and found nothing but wild grapes,— sad emblem of the sins and idolatries which ran wild in the heart of God's chosen and cherished people. In this tower of the vineyard were kept, in former days, and may still be seen, the various implements of husbandry, and all the means of pressing the grapes and making them into wine, so that it may be called "the farm of the vineyard." But the chief use of the tower, both in ancient and modern times, is as a dwelling-place and defence to the keeper of the vineyard, who, when the grapes are ripening, takes his station there, lest others should deprive him of the produce of his labor. McCheyne, describing the vineyards of Hebron, as he saw them in the year 1842, says, "They are of the most rich and fertile description, each one having a tower in the midst for the keeper of the vineyards. We were told that bunches of grapes from these vineyards sometimes weigh six pounds, every grape of which weighs six or seven drachms. Sir Moses Montefiore mentioned that he got here a bunch of grapes about a yard in length."

It is not possible for the reader of Scripture to have passed unnoticed the various allusions to the culture of the grape by the Hebrews. The great care which they bestowed on their vineyards, in selecting an appropriate spot of land for their growth, as well as in training the vine, is very apparent from the records of Holy Writ. Almost every part of Palestine is favorable to the culture of the grape; but the grapes of Eshcol, and Carmel, and Hermon, and the wines of Lebanon, were ever renowned for their sweetness, and are still unrivalled in the land of the sun. Sometimes the luxuriant plant hung its graceful festoons about the reed trellis; at others it clung from pole to pole, or clad the wooden palisade with a garment of verdure. Often, too, the vine-dresser directed its flexible branches over the side of the sunny wall, and then its boughs, as they ran over their support, suggested such images as lingered in the mind of the dying Jacob, when, describing the fruitfulness, and alluding to the protection given by his beloved son, he, in the figurative language of the eastern husbandman, said, "Joseph is a fruitful bough, even a fruitful bough by the side of a well; whose branches run over the wall."

Frequent and beautiful as are the poetic figures of the Old and New Testament, yet no object of nature furnished so great a variety of allusions as did the vine. Wherever the ancient Israelite looked around, there its broad leaves and wide-spreading boughs, and its purple clusters, caught his eye; and the holy prophet of old, and the Divine Saviour himself, ever ready to lead the mind from the fields of nature to the field of holy thought and spiritual communion, failed not to associate with it such lessons of joy and thankfulness, or of solemn admonition, as might recur again and again, in after ages, to him who walked in the vineyard. In the earliest parable of Scripture, that of the Trees choosing a King, we find the vine, in the language of allegory, exclaiming, "Shall I leave my wine, which cheereth God and man, and go to be promoted over the trees?" thus adverting to the use of wine in sacrifice, or to the first-fruit offering of the grape on the altar of God, as well as to its benefit to mankind. In that beautiful lament of forsaken Israel, expressed in Psalm lxxx., the writer portrays the sorrows of the church of God, under the image of a vine; and carries out, through a long succession, a series of figures so beautiful and touching, that he who now reads it mourns over ancient Israel's woes, and remembers, too, periods in the history of the Christian church when the vine seemed indeed trodden down, and when, for "a small moment," God "hid his face" from his people. "Once," says the sorrowing Asaph, "the hills were covered with the shadow of it, and the boughs were like goodly cedars. She sent out her boughs to the sea, and her branches unto the river. Now the boar out of the wood doth waste it, and the wild beast of the field doth devour it." And surely as we look upon God's ancient people, and see how their loved and holy city is trodden down of the Gentiles, we should breathe the aspiration of the Psalmist, "Return, we beseech thee, O God of Hosts; look down from heaven, and behold, and visit this vine; and the vineyard which thy right hand hath planted, and the branch that thou madest strong for thyself." In later days, our Saviour told his disciples, "I am the true vine, and my Father is the husbandman. As the branch cannot bear fruit of itself, except it abide in the vine; no more can ye, except ye abide in me." Then perchance he looked from the table, around which the disciples were gathered, and saw the graceful plant waving to the gentle summer wind, and putting forth its fruits for the vintage.

There is something pleasing in considering the Hebrew matron in the text as planting a vineyard for the use of her family. It was not enough for her that only what was absolutely needed should be supplied. She acted in the wise and beneficent spirit of the great Creator, who scatters, with liberal hand, not only the supply of our necessities, but the means of enjoyment; who charms the eye with verdure, and the ear with the songs of nature. We, in our northern climate, can scarcely form an idea of the value of the vineyard to an eastern family; the cooling shade of its overhanging boughs, in a land where the sun shines hotly through the long summer day, is indeed delightful; and in the Syrian vine-clad arbor, the Jewish families assembled, as do the natives of modern Palestine, beneath the vine and fig-tree. There, in pleasant groups, sitting in the soft air, we can fancy the pious mother, surrounded by her family, speaking with cheerful and thankful spirit of God's goodness to them all, and partaking together with them of the large clusters of yellow or purple fruits, gathered from the boughs. There lay the goodly cluster, and each took from it the welcome refreshment; and of the fruits which were to spare, the laborer gathered and packed in baskets, and probably laid, as they would do now, the broad palm-leaves above them, to preserve their coolness.

The month of October is that of the vintage; and on the hills once trod by the feet of the patriarchs the autumnal vintage is yet gathered. The Christian inhabitants of Lebanon, and other parts of Palestine, cultivate the grape for wine, both for themselves and for exportation; and the Moslems, as they do not drink wine, value the vine for its shadow, its fresh fruit, and for the raisins which they dry from it; besides that, vinegar is made from the grape, and the vine-leaves are eaten by cattle. This latter practice is referred to in the Jewish law, where Moses commands, "If a man shall cause a field or vineyard to be eaten, and shall put in his beast, and shall feed in another man's field; of the best of his own field, and of the best of his own vineyard, shall he make restitution." Chandler says of this practice in the East: "We remarked that about Smyrna the leaves were decayed or stripped by the camels and herds of goats, which are admitted to browse after the vintage."

Travellers who now visit the Holy Land are struck, however, with the desolate appearance exhibited by spots once famous for corn and wine, and the luxuriant vegetation of the East. God has turned "the fruitful land into barrenness, for the wickedness of them that dwelt therein." The old inhabitants of the land of the Hebrews are scattered as God predicted; and the thin population of strangers who now dwell there take little pains to cherish the soil. The want of agricultural industry is everywhere apparent; and he who loves the hill of Zion and the mountains about Jerusalem, because associated in his mind with all that is holy and all that is dear, longs for that glorious day when the Jews shall again be gathered under their native vines and fig-trees.

It is thought by most writers that the autumnal feast of Tabernacles, held by the Jews, had especial reference to the ingathering of the vineyard. "When ye have gathered in the fruit of the land, ye shall keep a feast unto the Lord seven days," were the words which enjoined this festival. The Syrian winter does not commence until December; and in that pleasant climate the month of October was well suited for the joyous out-door life which ancient Israel spent on this occasion. Then the song of praise and gratitude went up from the arbors formed of the "boughs of goodly trees, branches of palm-trees, and the boughs of thick trees, and willows of the brook." Then a loud burst of national thanksgiving was offered to the God who brought his people into a land flowing with milk and with honey; and every Jewish family brought its tribute of gratitude and praise.

SHE
GIRDETH HER
LOINS WITH STRENGTH,
AND STRENGTHENETH
HER ARMS.

SECTION VIII.

SHE GIRDETH HER LOINS WITH STRENGTH, AND STRENGTHENETH HER ARMS.

Reference is had, in this figurative expression, to the practice of girding tightly for any great exertion. The girdle which confines the loose and flowing garments of the native of the East is broad and long, and can, when occasion requires it, be bound several times round the waist and over the chest. This tight girding enables the men of oriental countries to perform wonderful feats of strength, especially in running; as they will make a journey of several miles, keeping pace with a horseman, or with the chariot of the great man. Sometimes the girdle is so tightly bound as to endanger life; and the editor of the "Pictorial Bible" mentions that he saw, at Ispahan, a pillar raised to mark the spot on which one of these tightly-girded runners expired, in attempting to stoop to the ground.

Scripture contains many references to this practice of girding. Thus we read, that when the prophet Elijah accompanied the bold and wicked king, "he girded up his loins, and ran before Ahab to the entrance of Jezreel." Even on occasions which demanded less exertion, it was usual to gather up the garment under the girdle, lest it might incommode the progress of the wearer. So our blessed Saviour represents the master as addressing his servant, "Make ready wherewith I may sup, and gird thyself, and serve me, till I have eaten and drunken;" and, when urging his disciples to a constant readiness for that spiritual warfare which they must encounter, and that watchfulness which the servants of the Lord must always exercise, he said, "Let your loins be girded about, and your lights burning; and ye yourselves like unto men that wait for their lord."

This figure of girding the loins would be especially expressive to the eastern, as well as to the ancient Greek and Roman people, among whom the practice prevailed. With the latter, it was considered very effeminate for a man to be seen abroad either without his girdle, or loosely girded, and tc be ungirt became an expression of an unmanly luxury. Sulla reproached Cæsar that he was ungirt; and Mæcenas was blamed because he wore his girdle loosely.

Boothroyd renders the passage,

> She girdeth up her loins for strength,
> And by exercise giveth vigor to her arms;

and it very evidently implies that she preserved her health by the very best means—that of cheerful and earnest employment. When we look at our bodily frames, and see how they are formed for exercise,—when we mark how the muscles of the active arm are firm, and those of the indolent soft and tender,—we see something of the bodily ills to which indolence exposes, and are convinced that a healthy frame can be preserved only by a due attention to activity; and when we mark, too, how painful and weary a thing sickness is, and how great is the physical enjoyment of health, it seems strange that exercise is so much neglected by thousands who have the means of taking it. How much exquisite enjoyment is afforded by the mere possession of health!—the pure taste, the high spirits, which render existence itself an enjoyment and a blessing, the good humor, the pleasure in innocent delights, the light and refreshing sleep, the appetite which needs no dainties, the untiring footstep, and the placid breathing, which scarcely quickens at the ascent of the mountain! O, if some of those of the female sex, who now spend their days on sofas, and their nights in unquiet dreams, would, like the excellent woman, strengthen their arms by exercise, and gird up their loins by some vigorous employment, how great a change should come over their constitutions, and how great a blessing should they gain for themselves!

There are also higher considerations than those of mere enjoyment which should induce us to cultivate the means of health. To do so is a religious duty. Health is one of the gifts which God has bestowed for usefulness — one of those talents of which he has said, "Occupy till I come;" and if it be wasted either by intemperance, indolence, or carelessness, we shall have to account for it at the great and solemn day of final retribution. If the hand of God deprive us of it, then may we calmly say, "The Lord gave, and the Lord hath taken away; blessed be the name of the Lord;" and appropriate the blessed promises to sufferers contained in Holy Writ; and while we remember that they also serve God who only stand and wait, we may learn many blessed lessons, when, like David, we can say, "Before I was afflicted I went astray; but now I have kept thy word." But if God has given us a robust constitution, or at least one that might, by exertion, be rendered such, then our very sickness is a sin. "Health," says Jeremy Taylor, "is the opportunity of wisdom, the fairest scene of religion, the advantages of the glorification of God, and the charitable ministries of men; it is a state of joy and thanksgiving, and in every one of its periods feels a pleasure from the blessed emanations of a merciful Providence. No organs, no lute, can sound out the praises of the Almighty Father so spritefully as the man that rises from his bed of sorrows, and considers what an excellent difference he feels from the groans and intolerable accents of yesterday." Health carries us to the place of worship, and helps us to rejoice in the communion of saints.

But though the text has an especial reference to

the strengthening of the body, yet that vigorous resolution inculcated by the apostle Paul may also be intimated here: "Wherefore," says the inspired writer, "gird up the loins of your mind, be sober, and hope to the end." A holy resolution, a moral courage, a steady determination in all things to obey the voice of conscience, seems a strong feature of the character of the Jewish woman. It is true that no resolution made in our own strength can avail us. Our hearts are sinful by nature, and ever ready to depart from God and holiness. Satan, like a roaring lion, seeking whom he may devour, is ever watching to hinder the progress of every right resolve. The world, with its anxious cares on the one hand, and its fascinating vanities on the other, is present with us to banish every pious motive, and drive us into forgetfulness and sinful weakness. Yet, unless we resolve rightly, we cannot act rightly; and there is a way of keeping the promise made to our own hearts and to God. There is a strength given to all who humbly ask it, in the name of the Great Mediator; a strength to will, to do, and to endure, even to the death; a strength, given by God, enabling the timid to be brave, and imparting a consistent firmness, even to those who feel themselves ready to be shaken by every breeze. But unless we seek from Heaven this consistent firmness of principle, our goodness shall be but as the morning cloud, and as the early dew that passeth away. Without it, no Christian course can be a happy or a useful one. It is not enough to know and approve what is right. Principle must be acted upon, whether the world smile or condemn; and the diligent and steady cultivation of firmness be sought in humble dependence on God. And as the eastern traveller girded his garments from the dust, so, too, must Christians keep themselves unspotted from the contamination of vain intercourse, and the defilement of sin; and as the Hebrew matron girded herself for strength, so should we strive to invigorate our principles by holy determination, by steady watchfulness, and by humble prayer; so that we may say with the apostle, "I can do all things through Christ which strengtheneth me."

"Weak as I am, yet, through thy grace,
I all things can perform."

SECTION IX.

SHE PERCEIVETH THAT HER MERCHANDISE IS GOOD; HER CANDLE GOETH NOT OUT BY NIGHT.

From the regular and constant industry for which the excellent woman is commended, it is evident that the work which she wrought, or which she superintended, would be of a good and valuable description. Diligence and perseverance in any pursuit give skill and taste in its performance, and enable the worker to excel one who is little interested in his work. Such a matron would, in time, become known and confided in for promptness and regularity, and for durable and beautiful workmanship; and, as Boothroyd renders the passage, "would see that her traffic is profitable." The tapestry, and girdles, and garments, all carefully woven and beautifully ornamental, would not disappoint the purchaser, who expected them, perhaps, to last a lifetime; and the maker would soon gain an established reputation among

PERCEIVETH THAT HER MERCHANDISE IS GOOD; HER CANDLE GOETH NOT OUT BY NIGHT.

those who bought, and thus in every way her merchandise would be good.

Archbishop Cranmer renders this verse: "If she perceives that her merchandise is good, her candle goeth not out by night." This might signify, that if, on any part'cular occasion, this Jewish lady saw some desirable object of purchase, she and her maidens would work long and diligently, even till night was far advanced, in order to procure it in exchange for her manufactures. Be that as it may, however, it is no uncommon thing, either in our own or other lands, for those engaged in manufactures to fulfil any large order by occasionally spending even a part of the night in its execution. In those eastern dwellings in which stuffs are made, there is great attention to business; and it sometimes occurs, that not only a busy group work from before the dawn till day is over, but that parties of workers are employed through the night, one party rising to work when the other retires to repose.

Dr. Clarke suggests that this burning of the lamp, however, implies rather a careful vigilance than a perpetual industry in the Hebrew mistress. He suggests that it was probably burned on account of the numerous banditti and lawless men, from various wandering tribes, who might come suddenly and endanger the family during the hours of darkness; and this caution to avert an ill, rather than to suffer it, well corresponds with the general character given by the description of the poem.

It appears to have been a very common practice among the ancient Hebrews, as it is now with nations of the East, for careful persons to burn a lamp by night in their dwellings. Candles are not burned in any oriental country, and therefore the word thus rendered refers to the lamp, of which we have so many notices in Scripture. Even as early as the time of Abraham we find a "burning lamp" mentioned, which appeared to him as a revelation from God. Gideon, when he led out his men against the host of Midian, bade them take their lamps in their pitchers; and from these early records of patriarchal times, even to the days of those whose pens concluded the pages of Holy Writ, we find the lamp and the oil continually referred to. Lamps were used in the tabernacle, and at marriage festivals were hung around the room, and cast down their light from above. Herodotus describes the lamps of the ancient Egyptians as "small vases, filled with salt and olive oil, in which the wick floated and burned during the whole night;" and as this description of the lamp exactly accords with the eastern lamp of modern usage, it seems probable that it was also a common form of the Jewish lamp. Many lamps, too, appear, like that of our engraving, to have had a small handle, for the convenience of removing them from place to place. Vegetable oil of some kind, and most probably exclusively olive oil, was burned by the Hebrews. Thus we find Moses commanding the Israelites to prepare the lamp for the tabernacle, which was to burn from evening to morning before the Lord: "Thou shalt command the children of Israel, that they bring thee pure oil olive beaten for the light, to cause the lamp to burn always." The wicks of the lamps were made of the coarser fibres of flax; and the Rabbins record, that the old linen garments of the priests were unravelled, to furnish those of the sacred lamps in the tabernacle.

The general use of the lamp naturally made it a frequent subject of metaphor and simile among ancient writers. Thus the wise man says, "The light of the righteous rejoiceth; but the lamp of the wicked shall be put out;" and again, the sudden extinction of the lamp served as a figure to express the wrath of God against him who cursed father or mother; for "his lamp shall be put out in obscure darkness." Many writers think that the expression "outer darkness," often used in Scripture, refers to the contrast of the outward darkness of night, when compared with that of the chamber in which it was so customary for the light to be burning. Our Saviour, addressing those who were accustomed to the highly poetic imagery of the east, spoke of the professor of piety under the figure of a lamp; and in the well-known and beautiful parable of the wise and foolish virgins, showed the danger of a careless and unwatchful profession of religion, commanding his followers to have their lights always burning.

In all ages, the lamp beaming from the chamber window on the dimness and gloom of the outward world, has awakened pleasurable and poetic associations in the mind of the traveller; and whether we are attracted by the small light of a cottage candle, seen from afar, or the still fainter lustre of an eastern lamp, yet our minds form some picture of the home within. The writer of the book of Proverbs, whose eye might rest on such a lamp, would imagine a home of industrious application. To him it would speak of care and vigilance; of the mistress and maidens gathered round it at their work; of children striving to lend a helping hand; and of a domestic scene of cheerful employment. To all of us such a lamp might seem like the hope which burns in the breast of one who loves and fears God. Now, perhaps, it burns feebly; some passing object dims its brightness, and suggests the idea of the worldly anxiety, or the sinful infirmity, which shadows that hope in the human bosom. Again, it rises into a bright and steady flame, cheering and gladdening all around it; and so the Christian's hope, soaring above these passing shadows, burns with its holy and life-giving lustre, shining brighter and brighter, till that perfect day of pure and unshadowed light. Perhaps it was after wandering in some lonely spot in the dimness of night, that David came upon some household lamp, and exclaimed, as it guided him onwards, "Thy word is a lamp unto my feet, and a light unto my path;" and while he blessed God for his holy word, added, "Thou shalt guide me with thy counsel, and afterwards receive me to glory." Our blessed Saviour said to his disciples, "Ye are the light of the world," and bade them, and us, for whom also his blessed words were spoken and afterwards written, so to let our light shine before men, that they, seeing our good works, might glorify our Father which is in heaven.

The dearest boon from Heaven above
  Is bliss which brightly hallows home;
'T is sunlight to the world of love,
  And life's pure wine, without its foam.
There is a sympathy of heart,
  Which consecrates the social shrine,
Robs grief of gloom, and doth impart
  A joy to gladness all divine.

Let others seek in wealth or fame
  A splendid path whereon to tread;
I 'd rather wear a lowlier name,
  With love's enchantments round it shed.
Fame 's but a light to gild the grave,
  And wealth can never calm the breast;
But LOVE, a halcyon on life 's wave,
  Hath power to soothe its strifes to rest.

SHE
LAYETH HER HANDS
TO THE SPINDLE, AND HER
HANDS HOLD THE DISTAFF.

SECTION X.

SHE LAYETH HER HANDS TO THE SPINDLE, AND HER HANDS HOLD THE DISTAFF.

Had not the sacred writer further enlarged upon the character of this woman, had this single praise been uttered of her, it would, to those for whom it was immediately intended, be of itself a high commendation. The Rabbins record and old saying of the Hebrews, that there is no wisdom in a woman but in the distaff; implying, as do the words of the text, that a woman's great praise is her industry. The Greeks and Romans would have accorded fully with the implied sentiment. When a Roman lady became a bride, she received many a hint, from the marriage ceremony, that she was about to enter on active domestic employment; and again and again the word *thalassio* resounded on her ear. This word, which signified the vessel in which were kept the materials for spinning, and the work already spun, reminded her, not only of the spindle and the distaff, to which it might directly refer, but was also significant of the various household occupations in which the women of ancient days felt it their duty and their honor to excel.

> "In those old times,
> There was far less of gadding, and far more
> Of home-born, heart-felt comfort, rooted strong
> In industry, and bearing such rare fruit
> As wealth might never purchase."

It was not until the more degenerate days of Rome, when luxury had supplanted the habits of the older state of society, that spinning and weaving were left to the slave. In earlier times, the bride went to her new home amid the throng of rejoicing maidens; and the young attendants carried in their hands the distaff and the spindle, with the gay colored wools hanging about them; — to all it spoke the same lesson,— the lesson so often inculcated by the Roman writers,— that a woman should resemble the bee for industry, and imitate Minerva, whose wisdom was so truly womanly in its direction, that she was said to be the first who ever wrought a web.

It was the pride of Augustus Cæsar, that his imperial robes, his fringed tunic, and costly girdle, were wrought in his household, by the hands of his wife, his sister, his daughter, and his grand-daughters. So, too, Alexander the Great, when advising the mother of Darius to teach her nieces to imitate the Grecian ladies in spinning wool, showed her the garments which he wore, and told her they were made by his sisters. The virtuous Lucretia worked with her maidens at the spinning-wheel; and Tanaquil, the wife of Tarquin, wrought woollen robes so well, that long after her death, her spinning implements, together with a robe of her manufacture, were hung up in the Temple of Fortune; a constant monument of her taste and skill, and an intimation to Roman maids and matrons that they, too, should lay their hands tc the spindle, and their hands should hold the distaff

The Jewish Scriptures so frequently refer to the

industry of women in occupations of this kind, that one can easily imagine the matron

> "At her wheel,
> Spinning amain, as if to overtake
> The never-halting time; or, in her turn,
> Teaching some novice of the sisterhood
> Her skill in this or other household work."

The ancient spindle or spinning-wheel was held by the right hand, and turned round, while the distaff or staff around which the wool was rolled was held in the bend of the left arm, and the thread drawn over the fingers of the left hand, so that both hands were employed.

The spindle and the distaff are the most ancient form of the spinning apparatus, and, in an improved condition, were long used even in our own country; hence the word spinster; and the English maiden or mother might often be seen sitting at her wheel

> "In summer, ere the mower was abroad
> Among the dewy grass — in early spring,
> Ere the last star had vanished."

But time has brought its wondrous improvements and great changes, and the well-constructed spinning machinery of modern days has banished from our cottage-doors the busy hum of the wheel. The cottager who once turned it gayly round has now to change her mode of industry, and has only to make up with her needle, into garments, the fabric which she would once have manufactured for herself.

But, besides the actual spinning or weaving of the wool and flax, the preparation of these substances gave much employment to the Jewish household. The flax required drying and preparing for use. The wool, after being combed and picked and carded, was put up in round balls, ready for the spindle. It was sometimes left for use with the natural moisture which fresh cut wool always yields, and which reminds us of the wool of Gideon's fleeces, out of which, in the Syrian climate, he could wring dew, "even a bowl full of water." Wool in this state was called plump-wool; but when the manufacturers were about to make some of those brilliant garments, whose tints no modern skill can furnish, the wool had to be subjected to the various processes of dyeing. In this case it was usual to anoint the wool with wine, or with some unctuous substance, preparatory to plunging it into the dye.

SECTION XI.

SHE STRETCHETH OUT HER HAND TO THE POOR; YEA, SHE REACHETH FORTH HER HANDS TO THE NEEDY.

Every reader of the Holy Scriptures must see how careful the great Jehovah has been, both under the old and new dispensation, to recommend to the care of the rich the wants of their poorer brethren. The law of Moses abounded in humane institutions respecting the poor, and these would be familiar to the Jewish woman. Though her Bible had not the Gospels, with their illustrations of the living and dying love of the Redeemer; though the sacred volume of the ancient Hebrew told not of the self-dying zeal of St. Paul, or other holy men of old, who lived and labored and suffered for others; though it had not the gentle and affectionate tenderness of the beloved disciple —yet its law made provision for kindness and humanity; and the poor and the destitute, the fatherless and the widow, were ever described as

SHE

STRETCHETH OUT HER HAND TO THE POOR; YEA, SHE REACHETH FORTH HER HANDS TO THE NEEDY.

the peculiar objects of God's love and compassion, and were recommended to the care of those to whom God had given wealth. "Blessed is he that considereth the poor · the Lord will deliver him in time of trouble," had been sung by the Psalmist; and still the words resounded in the tabernacle of the righteous, and still were met by answering feelings in the hearts of those who loved and feared Israel's God. It was in the exact spirit of the divine law that this woman acted. Moses had said, "The poor shall never cease out of the land; therefore I command thee, saying, Thou shalt open thine hand wide unto thy brother, to thy poor, and to thy needy, in thy land."

There is something very expressive in the figure of the text: "She stretcheth out her hand to the poor; yea, she reacheth forth her hands to the needy." It would seem to imply an attention to the wants of the poor, not forced upon her by immediate neighborhood. She waited not for the poor man to come to her door, but she went out to look for him. She did not deal out her bounty grudgingly, and by slow degrees, but gave with bounteous hands, and anticipated the duty taught afterwards: "Freely ye have received, freely give." She might have been seen, like Dorcas, making clothing for the poor, and distributing it with cheerful and willing kindness. She knew well that God loveth a cheerful giver. She was described as a woman "who feared the Lord," and his commands were her standard of duty. She would feel that the destitute ought to have a portion in all riches, so that God's blessing might rest on the wealth which she had gained. Such a woman could appreciate the kind and considerate command of her holy law, so suited to the agricultural habits of the people of a rich and fertile land: "When thou cuttest down thine harvest in thy field, and hast forgot a sheaf in the field, thou shalt not go again to fetch it; it shall be for the stranger, for the fatherless, and for the widow; that the Lord thy God may bless thee in all the works of thine hands. When thou beatest thine olive-tree, thou shalt not go over the boughs again; it shall be for the stranger, for the fatherless, and for the widow. When thou gatherest the grapes of thy vineyard, thou shalt not glean it afterwards; it shall be for the stranger, for the fatherless, and for the widow." And, whether it were the gleanings of her harvest field, or the wool of her flock, it was given with gladness. The poor who were near her rejoiced in her bounty, and the poor afar off were not forgotten. Even so may we see the ripplings of the waters around the pebble which is cast into the stream; and the ridges of water are fuller and larger nearest to the stone, and though they lessen as they recede, yet they form widening circles still, until they enclose the whole lake; just so were the deeds of love wrought by this woman, fullest in the charities of home, yet widening ever, until they encompassed the whole world in their embrace.

Dr. Adam Clarke considers the expression "needy" as applying especially to the afflicted poor. The poor whom sickness prevented from labor; the aged man, whose limbs refused to bear the weight of toil; the little child, too young to help himself; or the houseless stranger, who came to the gate of the Israelitish city to ask for succor; the latter had been especially commended to the pity of the ancient Hebrew: "Love ye therefore the stranger," said the Lord to his chosen people; "for ye were strangers in the land of Egypt." And he whom adverse circumstances had brought low was cared for in the humane precepts of the law. "If thy brother be waxen poor, and fallen in decay with thee, then thou shalt relieve him; yea, though he be a stranger or a sojourner; that he may live with thee.'

If we find it commanded as a duty and named as a praise, of the Hebrew woman, that she reached forth her hands to the poor and needy, how much more should this kindness to the indigent be expected of women reared in a country in which the gentle and loving spirit of the Gospel is fully known! The ancient duty of remembering the poor, so far from being abrogated by the New Testament, is enforced by more numerous and direct commands, and by the living example of our blessed Saviour, who "went about doing good."

One thing which must ever endear to the Christian his poorer brethren is the remembrance that Jesus Christ himself was the member of a poor family. The disciple of the Lord who had not where to lay his head, and who was supplied by the kind women who ministered to him, should feel a sincere pity and regard for the poor; for verily the Lord of glory took not upon him the nature of an angel; he came not with wealth or power, but made himself of no reputation, and for more than thirty years endured poverty and privation, that we might have everlasting happiness,—that to the poor the Gospel might be preached, and that they might be made "rich in faith, and heirs of the kingdom." In all the solemn and affectionate appeals made in God's holy word in behalf of the poor, there is not one which comes home more fully than this to the heart of God's children: "For ye know the grace of our Lord Jesus Christ, that, though he was rich, yet for your sakes he became poor, that ye through his poverty might be rich." O, if we could ever remember how short our time is for doing good,—that our sun may go down suddenly, while it is yet day; that if even the threescore years and ten of this mortal life should be allotted to us, it will be too short for half our projects,—surely we should hasten to-day to labor in God's vineyard; making sacrifices of time, and talents, and property, for the poor and needy of God's heritage, and laboring diligently ere the night cometh, when no man can work.

Nor must it be forgotten that on a Christian devolves the duty, not only of doing good to the body, but to the soul. Every one who has himself received the gift of God's spirit,—whose sins are pardoned through the Redeemer's grace,—is bound to study and promote the eternal welfare of others. Woe be to us, if our poorer brethren shall say, at the day of judgment, "No man cared for my soul." If we have the tongue of the learned, and can give good instruction, yet forbear to give it; if we can help the ignorant with a word of counsel; if we can bestow upon him the word of life, or induce him to join the assembly of God's earthly worshippers on the Sabbath day; if we can set before him a holy example; if we can send the missionary to the crowded alleys of our cities, or help him to traverse the wide waters to the dim and dark recesses of ignorance or cruelty,—and yet sloth, or carelessness, or self-indulgence, or parsimony, lead us to inertness,—then we are robbing those whom God has given into our care, and God will require their souls at our hands. But if we stretch out our hands to the needy, then may we hope for God's promised blessing, and our own spiritual wants will be supplied while we are aiding others.

There is also a peculiar feature in love to the

poor, which is impressed on the doctrines of the New Testament with greater distinctness than on those of the Old. Besides the general commands to love our poorer neighbor, we are especially "to do good to them who are of the household of faith." So much is this love to the disciples of Christ inculcated in the writings of the evangelists and apostles, that we are told we ought to "lay down our lives for the brethren." It is even made a test of our love to God. "Whoso hath this world's good," saith St. John, "and seeth his brother have need, and shutteth up his bowels of compassion from him, how dwelleth the love of God in him?" The contributions for the poor saints were not forgotten by the apostle Paul and the early Christians; and while it is the duty of Christians to do good to the bodies and to the souls of all, to stretch out the willing hand to the poor and needy, the poor of God's adopted family should be the especial objects of their love and care.

From Christ, the Lord, shall they obtain
Like sympathy and love again.

SECTION XII.

SHE IS NOT AFRAID OF THE SNOW FOR HER HOUSEHOLD: FOR ALL HER HOUSEHOLD ARE CLOTHED WITH SCARLET.

So accustomed are we to hear of the serene skies and genial warmth of the climate of Palestine, that we are, in our thoughts, apt to invest that interesting land with a perpetual sunshine. The flowery heights of the fragrant Carmel; the magnificent and enduring vegetation of Lebanon; the smiling plains of the still lovely and verdant Sharon; the grapes of Eshcol,—these are the features of the landscape most familiar to our mind. Although the cold of winter is not so severe as in some other parts of Syria, still it is scarcely less than that experienced in our own country. The autumnal shower is the early rain, for which the "husbandman long waited," that he might sow his seed; and in December, the first winter month, the rain falls in torrents, and the snow covers the plains occasion-

SHE
IS NOT AFRAID OF THE SNOW
FOR HER HOUSEHOLD; FOR
ALL HER HOUSEHOLD ARE CLOTHED
WITH SCARLET.

ally, and lies on the elevated mountains long after spring has made considerable advance ; while hoar-frost scatters its diamonds, or a mist, like that of our northern climates, obscures the face of nature.

Owing to the great inequalities of surface in the Holy Land, there are some sheltered and favored spots which are free from the cold of winter. Here the season is soft and mild, snow is seldom seen on the plains, and the orange-tree and the citron and the goodly palm contrast with the white summits and glittering icicles of Lebanon. On the mountains the snow is peculiarly deep from December, and scarcely decreases before the month of July. Dr. E. D. Clarke, speaking of one of the hills which forms a part of the majestic Lebanon, says: "The snow entirely covers the upper part of it; not lying in patches, as I have seen it, during summer, upon the tops of very elevated mountains,—for instance, that of Nevis in Scotland; but investing all the higher part with that perfect white and smooth velvet-like appearance which snow only exhibits when it is very deep ; a striking spectacle in such a climate, where the beholder, seeking pro tection from a burning sun, almost considers the firmament to be on fire."

We have various other instances in Scripture, besides that quoted at the head of the chapter, of the cold and snow of Palestine. The psalmist of Israel sung of the fleeces which the Creator "giveth like wool," and prayed that he might be purified, and made "whiter than snow." We infer the cold from the statement of the prophet Jeremiah, when he described Jehoiakim, king of Judah, as sitting with his nobles around the hearth, and daringly cutting with his penknife, and casting into the fire, the scroll which contained the denunciations of the Almighty. So again, in that sad hour, when the affectionate but frail apostle denied the Master whom he loved, we read that they had kindled a fire in the midst of the hall, and that Peter and others sat down together by it, "for it was cold."

The writer of the "Pictorial Palestine," describing the severe weather of January, says: "Major Skinner, who states that he traversed this country in a season unusually severe, speaks much of snow and cold. He mentions a village under Mount Carmel, in which many houses had been destroyed by the great quantities of snow which had fallen. He spent a night in that village, and on the morning of the twenty-eighth found the court-yard full of snow, which had fallen during the night. Snow was then resting on the ridge of Mount Carmel. Penetrating to the interior of the country, the same traveller reached Nazareth on the thirtieth. The heights around the town, and many of the houses, were covered with snow, large heaps of which were piled up in the court-yard of the convent. Many of the smaller houses had been destroyed by it; and the next day he found that the deep snow in the streets rendered it impossible to quit the city, and difficult to move about in it. A thaw had, however, commenced. The snow falls thick, and lies long on the mountains and high and intervening plains and valleys of Jebel Haouran, which may be said to bound eastward the country beyond Jordan. Madox found it so at the end of January. The same traveller, on the thirteenth, found Damascus covered with snow, as well as the mountains and plains round it."

Most commentators think that the Hebrew word rendered "scarlet" would be more correctly translated by the marginal reading, "double garments. It is thus rendered by Boothroyd in his version of Scripture, and the Septuagint and Arabic versions give it thus. The twice dyeing, which formed part of the process used in obtaining the brilliant scarlet of the East, caused this color to be expressed in the original language by the verb to redouble, and thus leaves the rendering in some measure doubtful. Dr. Adam Clarke states, in his commentary, that his old manuscript Bible renders this part of the passage "ben clothed with double;" and adds that Coverdale, with equal propriety, translates it, "For all hir household folkes are duble clothed." Whether we regard this double clothing as relating to an additional number of garments, put on during the winter season,—or whether we consider it as relating to a double stock of clothes, suitable for the winter, as well as the summer,—it still marks the care of her household shown by the mistress and the mother.

There are, however, some commentators who consider scarlet as the right rendering of the word from the original. Dr. Gill remarks, that if the word here used had been designed to be "double," it would have been in the dual number; and as this is not the case, he considers that in this, and similar instances, it is used for the scarlet color. He adds that both the Targum and Aben Ezra thus interpret it.

Supposing the word scarlet to be the correct translation in this passage, it would refer to the clothing provided by the Jewish matron for her husband and children only, and would not include the dress of her servants. Scarlet was a color much esteemed in the East, and the Jewish nobles and courtiers were accustomed, on state occasions and festivals, to wear robes of this brilliant dye. In that exquisitely touching lament, uttered by David over the fallen king, he exclaims, "Ye daughters of Israel, weep over Saul, who clothed you in scarlet, with other delights,—who put on ornaments of gold upon your apparel." So, too, Belshazzar was decked in the robe of scarlet; and when the prophet meant to contrast the wealth and luxury of Israel with its deepest degradation, he said, "They that were brought up in scarlet embrace dunghills." And now, in the land endeared to us by holiest associations, the bright coloring of the scarlet robe still attracts the eye of the traveller, in the winter season; and Lamartine speaks of the picturesque scarlet mantles of the Druses of Lebanon, and of the brilliant vests of scarlet velvet sometimes adopted by the Arab women.

If we keep to the latter rendering of the word, the passage would leave us simply to infer, that as the ordinary clothing of the family was that of the wealthier classes, there would not fail to be a provision of warm raiment prepared for the inclement season.

The ancient scarlet appears to have been sometimes a vegetable dye, obtained from the berries of a tree common in Canaan, and at others to have been procured from an insect resembling the American cochineal, though of a less brilliant tint. This insect, which was found chiefly on the leaves of the evergreen oak (*ilex aculeata*), was called by the Greeks and Romans *coccus*, but by the Arabs *kermes*, and from this latter word we derive our *crimson* and *carmine*. This scarlet dye is supposed to have been common in Egypt before the time of Moses, and to have been brought by the Israelites from that land. It is considered by most writers to be the scarlet named among the colors of the hangings of the tabernacle, by the cunning (or skilful) workman and embroiderer.

In the national character of the Hebrews, we can, through all ages, perceive the virtue of forethought, a characteristic which appears the more striking if we contrast it with the carelessness of the future exhibited by our warm-hearted neighbors, the Irish, or with the love of mere present gratification which marks the people of some continental nations. In the long series of cruel and oppressive acts, to which, in comparatively modern times, the ancient people of God have been subjected, this forethought has, in many instances, degenerated into a spirit of covetousness ; and the love of hoarding has been censured in the Jew by the very men whose rapacious tyranny turned this characteristic virtue into a vice. But the bright example of this pious woman, as portrayed by the Hebrew writer, under the direct inspiration of the Holy Spirit of God, is not that of a mean selfishness, not

"That strict parsimony
Which sternly hoarded all that could be spared
From each day's need, out of each day's least gain."

Hers was an enlarged and bounteous providence, one which, while it sought to guard against the ills, and provided for the comforts, of the coming days, while it gathered for her family enough and to spare, yet could have an open hand for the poor and needy. She acted on the principle of the charge given by the wise man to the sluggard, when he bade him consider the ways of the ant, "which provideth her meat in the summer, and gathereth her food in the harvest." She could give liberally to those who had nothing, while she avoided the censure afterwards pronounced by the apostle, "If any provide not for his own, and specially for those of his own house, he hath denied the faith, and is worse than an infidel." We have sometimes need to be reminded that prodigality is not generosity; that there is a prudent care for ourselves and others, which may consist in economizing present provision, so as to afford future comfort; and which is, as in the beautiful illustration of womanly virtue now before us, the result of a generous and enlarged thoughtfulness, which forgets not to consider the poor, nor neglects the enjoyment of present good.

Prudence is that necessary part of wisdom, which.

while it adapts its means to the end, refers chiefly to the prevention of ill. In looking to the future, we must see that evil of one kind or other waits us, if not met by a careful prudence. Even the warm and pleasant days of Palestine, its myrtles and roses, its many-tinted hues of sky,—all had to yield to the winter's snows, and coldness, and barrenness; and thus it is with our life itself. "The prudent man foreseeth the evil, and hideth himself; but the simple pass on, and are punished;" and the wretched fate of the imprudent man, whose want of consideration for the future leads him to poverty and ruin, is too often before us to be forgotten. But there is a worse evil to be prepared for than mere earthly poverty, and cold, and want, and suffering. Death is in itself an evil. Even the apostle could say, when speaking of the disunion of soul and body, "Not for that we would be unclothed." And if the Christian naturally shrinks from the prospect of death, though his life has been a preparation for heaven, and he knows that God will be with him in dying, O, how fearful must it be to him who in life never looked forward to his dying hour! The infidel is an imprudent man, for he hideth himself not from coming evil, but boldly defies the wintry hour of life. The worldly man is imprudent, for he sends forward no careful thought into the long future ; and though even our ages are but as a few waves from the great sea of Eternity, which ebb back again into that boundless ocean, yet he lives as if all our interests belonged to Time. The profligate man, who despises God, and loses in the sense of present gratification all consciousness of the evil which lies beyond, laments bitterly, on his dying bed, his neglect of the duty of forethought.

Forethought, however, must be distinguished from foreboding ; that cheerful calculation on future events, and providing against the vicissitudes of life, which are exemplified in the text, are wholly different from the dread of coming evil, the anxiety about sorrows which may never happen, which arises from a mistrust of the providence of God. Some people build castles in the air ; others seem intent on building dungeons. The over anxious mind is distrustful, and makes its owner miserable, when he ought calmly and happily to wait on God, and rely on his promises. To such might be applied the words of the poet:

> "Does each day upon its wing
> Its allotted burden bring?
> Load it not beside with sorrow
> Which belongeth to the morrow.
> Strength is promised — strength is given
> When the heart by God is riven:
> But, foredate the day of woe,
> And alone thou bear'st the blow."

SECTION XIII.

SHE MAKETH HERSELF COVERINGS OF TAPESTRY; HER CLOTHING IS SILK AND PURPLE.

Persons of wealth, in eastern countries, have ever been accustomed to dress in magnificent clothing, and to furnish their dwellings in a sumptuous and tasteful manner. There is, indeed, but little furniture in an oriental house. Couches and sofas, and hangings at the doors, are almost the only objects on which skill can be exercised, or which will admit the display of wealth in the possessor. In such a condition of society, it was certainly the duty of the wife of a Jewish magistrate, both to dress herself, and to array her house, in a style becoming the place and time. Had she done otherwise, she would have neglected the duties of her station, exposed her husband to censure, and herself have borne the reputation of a careless housewife. While to be clothed in silk and purple would be no praise of the modern female,

SHE MAKETH HERSELF COVERINGS OF TAPESTRY; HER CLOTHING IS SILK AND PURPLE.

in her it was significant of that sense of propriety which, in all ages, especially becomes the feminine character. The same duty of making home comfortable, of providing suitable furniture and clothing for the family, and of dressing according to her station, is practised by the excellent woman of modern times; and she who is not attired with a woman's neatness, and is indifferent even to the appearance of her house and family, has no claim to the reputation of a good wife, nor can she expect that her children will rise up and call her blessed.

The coverings of tapestry named in this passage refer probably to those embroidered quilted coverlets, used in all parts of Asia, for the divan or sofa. They might, however, signify carpets for her guests to sit upon; or those richly-worked curtains often hung at the oriental doorway, to keep the warm rays of the sun from entering the apartment; and which, separating the room from the beautiful garden into which it opens, yet admit the soft wind, laden with odors from shrubs and flowers. It seems most likely that these coverings of tapestry were worked with the needle, for although, in very early days, the Greeks and Romans used the loom in embroidering their tapestries, yet the practice of working by the needle was not only earlier, but was continued long after the introduction of the loom, and, indeed, to comparatively modern times. The Hebrews derived their skill in this art from the Egyptians, and among this people either the loom or the hand was employed in this kind of manufacture. Until within the last few centuries, much female skill and ingenuity have been bestowed on the working of tapestry, of which the celebrated Bayeux tapestry is a well known instance. This piece of needle-work, wrought either by the hand of Matilda, the wife of the Norman Conqueror, or worked by her maidens, under her direction, is a standing monument of feminine perseverance. It is twenty inches wide, and two hundred and fourteen long. It is worked in woollen threads, and resembles a large sampler; portraying, in figures somewhat uncouth, the various events connected with the Norman conquest.

The curtains of the Jewish tabernacle, described in the book of Exodus, "made of fine twined linen, and blue, and purple, and scarlet," are generally supposed to have been made of needle-work, in which the Jewish women are known to have excelled. Some of these curtains had precious stones and wires of gold worked in among the threads, as we see in the "clothes of service," and "holy garments," described by Moses. "And they did beat the gold into thin plates, and cut it into wires, to work it in the blue, and in the purple, and in the scarlet, and in the fine linen, with cunning work." That pictures describing various scenes of life or landscape were traced by female hands on their tapestries, there can be little doubt. Archbishop Cranmer translates the first and second verses of Exodus xxvi.: "Thou shalt make curtaynes of whyte twyned silke, yelowe silke, purple and scarlet. And in them thou shalt make pyctures of broidered work." The celebrated Babylonian tapestries were wrought with the needle, and represented either the mysteries of religion or some historical incidents; and the Greek and Roman ladies wrought embroideries which told to the eye a tale of hunting or war, of love or sorrow, and even in those early days wove tapestry little inferior to that which graces the halls of some of our old English castles and mansions.

The taste for brilliant coloring, so marked among the people of the East, seems a natural consequence of the bright hue of nature in the lands in which they reside; and the sober tints of our colder climate may have had their effect in moderating that taste in our own land. In countries in which the flowers are so brilliant that the flame itself seems hardly to exceed their brightness; where insects of ruby color or of brightest emerald unfold their wings; and birds varying in tint from every shade of purple to faintest azure fly among the trees,— there is a depth and richness of coloring to which our eye is unaccustomed. The amethyst sky at sunset; the very mountain peaks, tinged as they are, in some eastern lands, with hues of rose, and violet, and orange,—

> "For God has set his rainbows on them, while the cloud
> Lies at their feet:"—

These, when seen constantly, tend to impart to the taste a love for the bright and gorgeous tints which God has lent to color this earthly home. Blue, in every variety, was a favorite color with the ancient Hebrews. We find it mentioned continually in the decoration of the Tabernacle, and the dress of the priest; and it is generally thought to have been procured from indigo, which appears from the mummy cloths to have been used by the Egyptians, and was therefore doubtless known to the Jews. It is rather remarkable that in modern times this color is not esteemed in Palestine, nor admired as it once was, but has become connected with the idea of meanness, and worn only by the poorest of the people. But the purple was the color which appears to have had preëminence in ancient times, and which was so generally appropriated to kings and important personages, that even unto modern days the purple robe is emblematic of royalty. At a period early as that when Israel was ruled by judges, we find mention of this color, as worn by royal persons; and on that eventful day,

> "When grove was felled, and altar was cast down,
> And Gideon blew the trumpet, soul-inflamed,
> And strong in hatred of idolatry,"—

the kings of Midian appeared "clothed in purple raiment." It was, too, with the purple robe that Mordecai was decked, when he was promoted to honor by the Persian king; and to be clothed in purple and fine linen was the distinction of the rich man in the parable of the New Testament.

The purple mentioned in the text is believed by most writers to be the highly-valued Tyrian dye. This color was known in very ancient times, and prized, not only by the Hebrews, but by the Greeks and Romans. It was procured from two species of fish found on the shores of the Mediterranean and Atlantic seas; the one (*buccinum*) adhered to the rocks; the other (*purpura*) floated in the sea, and it was this species which afforded the dye most in request, and which is called in the Apocrypha the purple of the sea. From various varieties of these two species of shell-fish several tints of purple were obtained. The one was of a paler hue, and more resembling our scarlet; another was a deep violet tint, a color much valued by the Roman ladies in the time of Augustus; but the hue most admired was that deep purplish crimson which resembles clotted blood. This is said by Mr. Harmer to be the most sublime of all earthly colors, "having the gaudiness of red, of which it retains a shade, softened by the gravity of blue."

We can form some idea of the expensive nature of Tyrian purples, when we consider how large a number of shell-fish must be collected to furnish even a small quantity of the dye. These fish were sometimes two feet in length, but the only portion which yielded the color was a small white vein in the neck; so that a number of fishermen must have been employed for many days, before they could obtain enough to color even a single garment. The art of dyeing the Tyrian purple is now lost; but it is probable that its place is well supplied by the rich hues of vegetable dyes employed in modern times.

The Rev A. Bonar and Robert McCheyne, who lately visited the Holy Land, on a mission of inquiry respecting the Jews, remark of the shore near the bay of Acre: "We saw some of our neighbors seeking for specimens of the shell-fish from which, in ancient times, used to be extracted the famous purple dye. We did not find any specimens, but were told it is still to be found there. It used to be found in all parts of the bay, and there were two kinds of it. One of these yielded a dark blue color, the other a brighter tint, like scarlet; and by mingling these two juices, the true purple color was obtained." "It was thus," adds the writer, "that Asher, whose rich and beautiful plain supplied viands fit for the table of kings, yielded also the dye of their royal robes, conveyed to many a distant coast by the merchants of Tyre and Sidon, and thus we see the full meaning of Jacob's blessing on Asher, 'He shall yield royal dainties.'"

The great use of the purple color among the wealthy classes of the Hebrews gave employment to many of the Tyrian merchants. Thus we find that when Ezekiel addressed Tyrus, in the language of prophecy, he referred to it: "Syria was thy merchant by reason of the multitude of the wares of thy making; they occupied in thy fairs with emeralds, purple and broidered work." In later ages, we read of a very interesting character, Lydia, who was "a seller of purple" at Thyatira, whose "heart the Lord opened, that she attended unto the things which were spoken of Paul," and whose warm and earnest love to the apostle and his companions urged her to constrain them to dwell in her house; and this rich color, in which the matron of the text is said to be clothed, was probably one of those species of merchandise which she is said, "like the merchants' ships, to have brought from afar."

Her
HUSBAND
is known in the gates,
when he sitteth among
the elders of the land.

SECTION XIV.

HER HUSBAND IS KNOWN IN THE GATES, WHEN HE SITTETH AMONG THE ELDERS OF THE LAND.

Greatly indeed is it to the credit of a woman, that her husband should be known and honored for her sake; that in the places of public resort he should be recognized as the husband of a wife, who so arranged the household duties, and took so practical a part in the concerns of the family, that he was enabled to devote his time to public business. His dress, too, ever becoming his station, and wrought with industrious skill in his own home, would be noticed in an oriental assembly; while an unspotted reputation, gained by a virtuous and consistent life, reflected its lustre on all connected with the Jewish woman.

And as it was in the days of old, so is it now, that whatever position in life we may occupy, we cannot stand alone. Whether individual conduct bring disgrace or win respect, others must share in it. So, too, we all must influence others; and of all means of moral influence, none is greater than that of a good reputation. Without it, indeed, all good influence is lost. The Scripture proverb says, "A good name is rather to be chosen than precious ointment;" and, for the preservation of this good name, a woman's conduct must not only be marked by integrity and simplicity, but it must be steady and uniform. The very shadow of ill, the very appearance of evil, is to be shunned by every woman professing godliness; and in the eye of the world she should be blameless, approving herself not only unto God, but also unto men.

When we find it implied that a woman's character brought an honor to her husband, we are quite sure that it was marked by consistency. This can be the result only of the possession of good principles, and of a determination, by the grace of God, to make these principles the basis, not only of every important duty, but of the minor acts of life. It must proceed from a high and enlarged sense of responsibility, and was never yet attained by any who had not seriously studied her own particular duties, and cultivated also the duty of firmness.

We all rely fully on a consistent person, and instinctively value his opinion. Every one must have seen that there are some, who, without attempting to gain influence over others, yet possess it to so great a degree, that even vice stands abashed in their presence : the swearer will fear to utter his oath, the drunkard will feel ashamed of his sin, and the frivolous will stay his folly. Even the little child recognizes consistency, and feels the force of reproof or praise uttered by its possessor. It is remarkable, too, that our characters are generally read fairly, and well understood, by those around us. Weight of character never fails to make its due impression. We are judged, not only by the expression of our sentiments,—for in these we might deceive,—but by the hourly acts which make up human life, the impulse which prompts the unconsidered word, the very look which betrays the thought ; the little things, which in their individual manifestation seem nothing, yet the amount of which makes up our character, and causes it to be rightly read.

The ancient custom of holding meetings for public justice under the gateway of the town, as well as the reference to the elders, leads us to the conclusion that the husband of the Jewish woman held some office of public trust. As early as the time of Abraham, we find business transactions performed in the gate, when the patriarch purchased the cave of Machpelah, in the audience of Heth; and the silver was weighed in the presence of all them that went in at the gate of the city. And Boaz bought of Naomi the land of his family, in the presence of the witnesses at the gateway, and of the elders. The convenience of the gate, as being not only a regular place of thoroughfare in and out of the city, but a public place of resort, rendered it peculiarly suitable for the transfer of property, at a time when written documents were little known, and the transaction had consequently to be attested by several of the inhabitants of the neighborhood. Homer states of the Trojans, that their elders assembled in the gate to judge of the rights between man and man.

In the law of Moses we find direct reference to the practice of holding law-courts in these entrances to towns. "Judges and officers shalt thou make thee in all thy gates, which the Lord thy God giveth thee, throughout thy tribes; and they shall judge the people with just judgment." And when Job looked back on more prosperous days, and compared with them his state of present sorrow, he says: "When I went out to the gate through the city, when I prepared my seat in the street! the young men saw me, and hid themselves; and the aged arose, and stood up;" while the mournful Jeremiah predicted, as one of the signs of desolation on his native land, that the elders should cease from the gate.

But beside the business of judging the people of Israel, and of conveying estates or other property, the gateway was often a market-place; and there were assembled the merchants who trafficked in the various goods of the East. Thus we find Elisha announcing to the famished people of Samaria, "To-morrow shall a measure of fine flour be sold for a shekel, and two measures of barley for a shekel, in the gate of Samaria."

It can easily be imagined that a place of such great concourse would become a resort, not only for men of business, but for men of leisure; and the oriental gateway held the same place in the town which is now occupied by the coffee-house. There neighbors met to talk over the affairs of the city, to speak of the past, and to speculate on the future; to dwell on the faults of their fellow-townsmen, or to expatiate on their worth. If any man wished to meet with his neighbor, he went up to the gateway; if he had public news to communicate, he carried it thither. If he wished to attract the notice or to win the ear of the governor of the city, he would sit, day by day, as Mordecai did, in the king's gate. So, too, we find Isaiah speaking of him "that reproveth in the gate;" and Jeremiah delivered his solemn warnings and commands "in the gate of the children of the people;" and it was when the Psalmist felt that he had become the object of the unjust reproaches of his neighbors, that he said, "They that sit in the gate speak against me."

It does not appear that the assembly of people who thus met in the gateway formed any hindrance to the passing of the towns-people in and out of the city. In eastern gateways, in the present day, there is a slightly raised seat on both sides of the arch, and under the pleasant shadow of the wall the man of the East still lounges and chats, and receives company. Such accommodation no doubt belonged to the Hebrew gate. There are, besides, on each side of some gateways, open rooms or cells in the walls of the gate, in which a number of people sit during the greater part of the day.

It was because of the publicity of the Hebrew gateway, that the Lord commanded the ancient Israelite to write upon it the words of his holy law. Texts of the sacred book were ordered to be transcribed upon the posts of their houses, and upon their gates, that all Israel might continually be reminded of the Great Jehovah, and of his high and holy commands. The laborer, as he went forth to his fields and his vines, looked up to the written words, and the merchant's busy thoughts of gain were sometimes arrested and brought into a different course. Many a pious Israelite regarded them with love and reverence, and perhaps, like David, thanked God for them, and could exclaim, "Thy word is very pure; therefore thy servant loveth it;" and often they suggested thoughts of prayer, or led the mind of the pious Jew forward to the Great Messiah, who should come one day to fulfil all those solemn types and shadows which the law now set forth, and who should, under a more glorious dispensation, himself magnify the law, and make it honorable.

"What I most prize in woman
Is her affection, not her intellect.
Compare me with the great men of the earth—
What am I? Why, a pigmy among giants!
But if thou lovest,—mark me, I say lovest,—
The greatest of thy sex excels thee not!
The world of the affections is thy world—
Not that of man's ambition. In that stillness
Which most becomes a woman, calm and holy,
Thou sittest by the fireside of the heart,
Feeding its flame. The element of fire
Is pure. It cannot change or hide its nature,
But burns as brightly in a gypsy camp
As in a palace hall."

SHE,

MAKETH
FINE LINEN, AND
SELLETH IT; AND DELIVERETH
GIRDLES UNTO THE MERCHANT.

SECTION XV.

SHE MAKETH FINE LINEN, AND SELLETH IT; AND DELIVERETH GIRDLES UNTO THE MERCHANT.

Biblical critics have carefully studied the Hebrew word here translated "fine linen." Woollen garments seem to have formed the chief articles of dress among the ancient Jews; but both in Egypt and Syria garments were also worn of fine linen and cotton, as well as of a substance called *byssus*. This latter material seems to have been a fabric of fine muslin—one of those "webs woven of air," which in India are worn at the present day, and which the Hindoo ladies wrap around them in numerous folds of drapery. It seems probable that persons of wealth and distinction in Canaan, as well as the priests and Levites, wore garments of fine linen, white or dyed; made of the linen manufactured either in Egypt, or of an inferior quality made in the Jewish household, such as was wrought by the excellent woman in the text.

The general culture of flax in Palestine, the statement that the women spun it for the hangings of the tabernacle, and the still more immediate fact that this woman, when she worked willingly with her hands, sought flax as well as wool, leads us to infer that in this passage at least the rendering of linen rather than silk or cotton is the true one. Although, according to the Talmudists, the ancient Hebrew wore a woollen garment next his skin by day, yet cleanliness and comfort rendered it necessary that the nightly dress should be made of linen, and this appears to have been the general practice. Many of the robes of purple, scarlet, blue, and other colors, of which we read, appear to have been of a linen fabric.

But this word is thought by some writers to imply a loose inner garment, generally worn in the East — a kind of shirt. Kimchi thinks the word signifies a night-covering, and considers that it ought to be translated "linen sheets." "The Arabic," says Dr. Clarke, "gives a remarkable rendering of this verse: 'She maketh towels or table-cloths, and sells them to the inhabitants of Bozra,— a city of Mesopotamia,—and fine linen, and sells them to the Canaanites.' " Kitto concurs with the Rabbi in thinking that the word here used describes either sheets, or else under garments made of linen. It is the same as is rendered sheets in the book of Judges, where Samson promised thirty sheets and thirty changes of raiment, as a reward for guessing his riddle. It is not at all probable that in this latter case sheets are intended, because, when Samson slew thirty Philistines near Ashkelon, it is hardly to be supposed that they were carrying their bed-clothes with them. Besides, they would, like all other eastern beds, have had two sheets, and therefore thirty would have provided twice the number required, while the shirts taken from the bodies of the slain would have exactly supplied Samson with the means of performing his promise.

As no pictures or monuments have descended from the people of Israel to the modern Jew, we have no definite means of ascertaining their mode of dress. Scripture allusions form our chief guide, but tradition, as well as the costumes figured on the monuments of the other ancient nations of the East, and the present mode of dress in Egypt and the Holy Land, afford some assistance. It is still customary for the Bedouin to wear a cotton or woollen shirt or frock, generally fastened round the waist with a girdle. This is often, in summer, the only dress of the poor, and is the usual in-door dress even of the wealthy class of society. In winter, persons of humble condition wear over this garment the woollen mantle or "hyke," a kind of dress very similar to the plaid of the Scottish Highlander. The hyke may be described as a large woollen blanket, serving as a covering both for day and for night; and was, most likely, the garment referred to in that humane provision of the law, where, if the Israelite took a pledge of his poorer brother, he was enjoined: "In any case thou shalt deliver him the pledge again when the sun goeth down, that he may sleep in his own raiment, and bless thee; and it shall be righteousness unto thee before the Lord thy God."

The Talmud enumerates eighteen several garments, as forming the dress of the ancient Israelites; and it is evident from Scripture, that many robes and garments were worn by the rich, though the frock and mantle might serve for the poor.

That fine linen was worn only by persons of distinction in Canaan, is very apparent, from the value attached to it, and the comparisons it suggested. When the beloved apostle John wrote, in the isle of Patmos, that solemn revelation of prophecy, so much of which yet remains unfulfilled to the church and to the world, the fine linen, pure and white, presented to his mind an image of the righteousness of the redeemed church. "And to her," says he, "was granted that she should be arrayed in fine linen, clean and white; for the fine linen is the righteousness of saints,"—that spotless robe wrought by the Saviour, for every child of God, redeemed from among men by the blood of the Lamb, sanctified by his Spirit, and made meet for tuning the golden harp of the celestial city,—that robe, of which the Saviour says, "I counsel thee to buy of me white raiment, that thou mayest be clothed;" lest, being unclothed, the sinner should find, at the great day of God's judgment, that he was "poor, and miserable, and blind, and naked," having nothing in which to appear but his own righteousness, which the Scripture has declared to be, in the sight of God, but as "filthy rags."

In a house in which the manufacture of various tissues seems to have been carried on so diligently as in that of the excellent woman, linen enough would be wrought for traffic. Both this and the girdles were probably sold, not only to the merchants of her own city, but also to the Canaanites, or Phœnicians, who traded with them to Egypt and other distant lands, which their ships visited.

The continual reference to the girdle in Scripture establishes the fact, that among the ancient Hebrews it was considered as necessary an article of attire as it is in the present day in oriental countries. Its use in girding the loins for exertion has been already referred to, but it served also for various other purposes. The ancient Jews are supposed to have worn two girdles,— the one around the body, under their inner garment, the other around their outer dress. It was this latter girdle which was tightened for exercise. The wealthy Jews, who evidently paid much attention to dress, no doubt prided themselves upon the taste and manufacture of this portion of it. In the present day, the Arabs wear, as a girdle, an embroidered shawl, or a figured muslin, and the girdle is a piece of outward finery throughout the East. Sometimes it is beautifully wrought with colored wools or silks, shells, beads, etc Among the poorer classes, leathern girdles are still worn, and probably differ little from that with which John the Baptist fastened his camel's-hair garments. Leathern girdles are also worn by the richer Arab, when he prepares his dress for a journey.

The girdle most commonly worn by the ancient Hebrews was probably made of woollen fabric, skilfully wrought by woman's hand with embroidered patterns. It folded several times round the body, and confined the floating garment. One end of this girdle was doubled back, and sewn at the edge, so as to form a purse; and was most likely referred to by our Saviour, when, sending forth his apostles on their holy mission of love, he said, "Provide neither gold, nor silver, nor brass, in your purses." The Romans and Greeks also formed their purses by the folding of the girdle, and there carried their money. Paxton quotes the saying of C. Gracchus, in Aulus Gellius: "Those girdles which I carried out full of money, when I went from Rome, I have, at my return from the province, brought home empty." Forbes mentions that the Mahrattes of the present day generally carry in their leathern girdles, covered with velvet, their most valuable papers and precious jewels.

It appears from the Scriptures, that the ancient Hebrews, like the modern Turks, wore a poniard or sword in their girdle; for we read, "And Joab's garment that he had put on was girded unto him, and upon it a girdle with a sword fastened upon his loins in the sheath thereof, and as he went forth, it fell out." This practice must not be understood as designed for a cruel and revengeful purpose, but originated in the want of knives. The Turkish secretary, or writer of modern days, substitutes for this weapon in his girdle the ink-horn and the pen; and it seems probable that those among the Jews whose employments were of a literary character wore ink-horns in their girdles. Thus we read in Ezekiel of one who was clothed with linen, and had an ink-horn by his side. The pens too are placed in the girdle, and the ink-horn is firmly closed with a clasped lid.

The manufacture of girdles for the merchants would, of course, employ many hands. When we consider, too, that girdles, as well as robes, are in request for presents all over the East, this alone requires a great supply. The Rev. W. Jowett has said that the two words "give, give," might very properly be taken as a motto to the armorial bearings of Syria. No one would think of appearing before a great man without a present in his hand: as says the proverb, "A man's gift maketh room for him, and bringeth him before great men;" and the habit of giving gifts, especially of various parts of the dress, extends itself to the most ordinary occasions. The gift of a girdle from a warrior was evidently a great mark of friendship. Among the Greeks and Romans also it was thus considered. When Hector and Ajax ceased from the combat, in which they had encountered each other, Hector gave his girdle to Ajax, as a token of amity. In the book of Samuel we find Joab blaming the man who saw Absalom hanging in the wood, in these words, "Why didst thou not smite him there to the ground? and I would have given thee ten shekels of silver, and a girdle." Jonathan, too the "lovely and pleasant" Jonathan, when about to certify the covenant made between himself and his friend, gave, among other things, his girdle to David; and even to the present day, the girdle is often loosed and given to one who is beloved. "And Jonathan stripped himself of the robe that was upon him, and gave it to David; and his garments, even to his sword, and to his bow, and to his girdle."

"She, while her husband toiled in state affairs,
Eased him of all his economic cares;
In all that bounded was within her sphere,
Her wisdom shined, in her whole conduct clear;
No vain expense she on herself bestowed,
A spirit frugal and yet generous showed;
She of God's blessings could no waste endure,
But in rewards was bountiful and sure;
The poor had an allotted liberal share
In all that she with decency could spare.
Her usual dress was comely, never gay,
No new vain fashion could her judgment sway;
Her speech was uncensorious and restrained, —
All that she spake a pleased attention gained."

STRENGTH

AND HONOR ARE
HER CLOTHING, AND
SHE SHALL REJOICE IN TIME
TO COME.

SECTION XVI.

STRENGTH AND HONOR ARE HER CLOTHING; AND SHE SHALL REJOICE IN TIME TO COME.

No one can fail to see that the character ascribed to this woman, especially the stability of her conduct, and the good reputation which it gained her, render this figure sufficiently expressive. She was, indeed, clothed in strength and honor, and might well rejoice in coming days. For old age she had prepared something more than a store of mere worldly good. She had not only been provident of present wealth, and wrought such works as time should not easily injure,—such as she should not blush to acknowledge as hers in future time,—but she had laid up in the hearts of her husband and children, and the poor and needy, a treasure of love, which time should not change. Above all, if the days should come when, in the figurative language of Solomon, the grasshopper should be a burden, and desire should fail, and the almond-tree should blossom, her help and stay would be on God, her hope and trust in heaven, and the joy of the Lord should be her strength. He who had sustained her through the active period of life,—who had kept alive in her heart his love and fear at a period when temptations from outward circumstances and inward feelings were great,—would not fail her in days when exertion would become toil, and when the desire of rest had taken the place of pleasure in her heart: for he had said, "Even to your old age I am he; and even to hoar hairs will I carry you."

How beautiful and graceful is the repose of the aged servant of God! How placid the mental rest and assurance of one who has served God from youth upward! The Christian graces, mellowed by time, shine now with a mild and settled lustre; and the meek waiting upon God diffuses over the later hours of life its calm and steady light, like the soft tints which the moon casts on the tranquil sea. Every one too must rejoice, who has been enabled, by God's grace, to maintain through life a consistent profession of holiness; and to have spent the days in useful employment must bring to old age its pleasant recollections. No self-gratulation would indeed fill the pious mind, on a review of the past. "Not unto us, O Lord, not unto us, but to thy name" be the praise, would be the exclamation of one who opened her mouth with wisdom; but she would trace with thankfulness how God had led her all her life through the wilderness; how he had placed her in a land where his ordinances were known, and his name honored; and had enabled her to conduct her household in the fear of the Lord, and to provide them with every temporal and spiritual good. For such blessings she would rejoice in the time to come, in the season of gray hairs; for such pleasant remembrances, she would lift up her heart to God and be thankful.

But the time to come may have reference to the day of death,— to that solemn hour of final parting with earth,— to that glorious moment of entering heaven; and at a period when the worldly woman might shrink with fear, she might rejoice in the Lord. For David sang, and the response to his harp has been echoed by millions of God's children in the last hour,— "Yea, though I walk through the valley of the shadow of death, I will fear no evil for thou art with me; thy rod and thy staff they comfort me." Leaning on this staff, how many pious men and women of all ages have entered the valley, singing as they went! Many years before this time, Jacob had said, on his dying bed, "I have waited for thy salvation, O Lord;" and Job, full of a fervent faith, had exclaimed, "I know that my Redeemer liveth, and that he shall stand at the latter day upon the earth; and though after my skin worms destroy this body, yet in my flesh shall I see God." We have not recorded for us the last breathings of Moses; yet how calmly and cheerfully did he resign his breath! And when the Lord bade him go up alone to Mount Nebo, and to die there, after having given his last glance to the promised land, what was his testimony of his heavenly Father? "Yea," said the dying saint, "the Lord loved his people;" and looking up to God, he added, "all his saints are in thy hand:" and thus he rejoiced in God, when heart and flesh were failing. "Ah!" said a holy woman, known to the writer, "in a few moments I shall be in heaven; I have nothing to do now; I am only waiting: O how I long to be released! Christ is with me; nature may fail, but he never will."

The "time to come" may also have reference to eternity,—to the unending myriads of years to be spent in the presence of God,—to the days of glory to be passed in that heavenly city, to which the pious Jew, as well as the Christian, was tending, where the inhabitant shall no more go out. And who shall describe or imagine the joys of heaven? What earthly tongue shall tell of the rejoicing in that time to come, when the Lord shall say, "Well done, thou good and faithful servant, enter thou into the joy of thy Lord"?

"Hath she not soothed me sick, enriched when poor,
And banished grief and misery from my door?
Hath she not cherished every moment's bliss,
And made an Eden of a world like this?
When care would strive with us his watch to keep,
Hath she not sung the snarling fiend to sleep?
And when distress hath looked us in the face,
Hath she not told him, thou art not disgrace?"

SECTION XVII.

SHE OPENETH HER MOUTH WITH WISDOM; AND IN HER TONGUE IS THE LAW OF KINDNESS.

Delighted, we turn from the contemplation of the active duties of this Jewish matron, to the gentle graces which adorn her character. So many proofs of practical judiciousness are exhibited in this portraiture, that we are not surprised to find that she also opened her mouth with wisdom. It is, however, a most difficult part of self-government to guard the tongue. The apostle James recognized this, when he said, "If any man offend not in word, the same is a perfect man, and able also to bridle the whole body." And yet how important a medium of good or ill is conversation! The children in a household gather instruction not only from direct teaching, but from the casual expressions to which they listen. A word spoken in due season, how good is it! and happy are they, who form part of the domestic

SHE

OPENETH HER MOUTH WITH WISDOM;

AND IN HER TONGUE IS THE LAW OF KINDNESS.

circle of one whose piety and experience of life enable her to give wise counsels, and to utter sentiments of justice and truth.

The wisdom for which this woman is commended related not alone to the things of the present world. She was one who feared the Lord. She could tell to her listening household of the wonders of nature; and of the deliverances wrought by God's providence to ancient Israel, how he brought them through the Red Sea, and out of the land of bondage, and gave them the promised country. She could point to the infallible laws of nature, and show that the morning sun and the evening star never disappointed him who watched for them in the heavens. She could point to the lily of the field, which bloomed at its appointed season, and to the swallow which knew the time of its coming, and infer from them that he who gave his written promise would as assuredly fulfil this also. She could discern in the types and figures of God's law the shadows of a more glorious future; and the promise of Messiah, the Hope of Israel, who was to bring comfort and holiness to the church of God, was a living fountain of joy in her bosom. Doubtless, too, she could tell of family and individual mercies; for God never implanted his fear in any human heart, but in that heart was awakened a chord of love and gratitude, which excited it to praise. She could remind her children of God's solemn commands, and, speaking of the saints of older times, could bid them to be "not slothful, but followers of them who through faith and patience inherited the promises." Hers was the wisdom described in Scripture as that which cometh from above, which is "first pure, then peaceable, gentle, and easy to be entreated, full of mercy and good fruits, without partiality and without hypocrisy."

But the wisdom of the Jewish woman related not alone to the things of our better life; it took cognizance also of the affairs of this. While she did not always speak of the things of religion, she spoke always as a religious woman, as one who felt the responsibility of life and duty.

> "Methinks we see thee, as in olden times,
> Unmoved by pomp or circumstance, — in truth,
> Inflexible, and with a Spartan zeal
> Repressing vice and making folly grave.
> Thou didst not deem it woman's part to waste
> Life in inglorious sloth, — to sport a while

Amid the flowers, or on the summer wave,
Then fleet, like the ephemeron, away;
Building no temple in her children's hearts,
Save to the vanity and pride of life
Which she had worshipped."

The wisdom with which this woman opened her mouth was most likely that derived from experience of life, from thought and observation, and a knowledge of her own heart. It was something better than mere learning, and did not consist in a simple acquaintance with facts. Facts, with such a woman, would form the basis of intelligent thought; and while her wisdom would not be opposed to cheerful converse and the play of fancy, it would discountenance sin and folly, and all profane jestings or irreligious allusions, and qualify her to give good counsels as a mother in Israel.

"Knowledge and wisdom, far from being one,
Have ofttimes no connection. Knowledge dwells
In heads replete with thoughts of other men;
Wisdom, in minds attentive to their own.
Knowledge, a rude, unprofitable mass,
The mere material with which wisdom builds,

> Till smoothed and squared, and fitted to its place,
> Does but encumber whom it seems to enrich.
> Knowledge is proud that he has learned so much,
> Wisdom is humble that he knows no more."

It is a beautiful and appropriate praise of woman, that on her tongue is the law of kindness. When we look on this fallen world, and see what misery has been brought into it by sin; that the storm, and the famine, and poverty, and sickness, bring sufferings which none can avert, and when we see, too, that there exist sorrows deeper still than these, and hear the expressions wrung out from hearts full of anguish, — how strange does it seem, that any should add to the afflictions of life by a want of kindness, or aggravate by cruel words the bitterness with which the heart is already breaking! And if the sorrows of life demand sympathy and help from every member of the human family, — if it is by bearing one another's burdens that we are to fulfil the law of Christ, — surely there is an especial claim on woman for deeds and words of kindness. On her devolve all the tender offices of life. To her care is given the frail and helpless infant, needing from the hour of its birth all that deep and earnest solicitude, and patience, and self-denial, which God has provided for in the richness and fulness of maternal love. In her charge, too, is placed the simple child, with its questionings of wonder and its innocent confidence; needing the exercise of love and tenderness, to restrain the sinful propensities of its nature, and to lead into the paths of peace. And where is woman's kindness more often needed, or more often seen, than in the chamber of sickness? It is hers to watch through days and nights by the couch of suffering; to tread so softly as not to disturb the lightest sleep; to anticipate every want; to bear patiently with the irritability of pain; and to minister relief with a tact and unweariedness to be found nowhere so securely as in woman's love. It is often woman's lot, too, to point the dying man to that atonement for sin which the death of the Saviour has provided; and frequently, in dwellings where the foot of the man of God may not have found its way, she may be found bringing the joyful tidings of salvation to the repentant sinner.

"O woman! though thy fragile form
Bows like the willow to the storm,

Ill suited in unequal strife
To brave the ruder scenes of life;
Yet, if the power of grace divine
Find in thy lowly heart a shrine,
Then, in thy very weakness strong,
Thou winn'st thy noiseless course along;
Weaving thine influence with the ties
Of sweet domestic charities,
And softening haughtier spirits down,
By happy contact with thine own."

God has provided for woman's duties by endowing her with the faculties which tend to their performance. He has given the quick sensibility; the lively imagination, which helps her to guess, by a word or glance, at the feelings of others; and, in most cases, a warm devotion to those whom she loves; and it cannot be denied that impulses of kindness are generally found in the female sex. It remains for a holier motive than mere human feeling to make this kindness constant and enduring; and it needs a sense of duty, derived from a consideration of love to God, to enable woman to be kind always, and be kind to all, even her enemies, and especially to let all her words be governed by the law of kindness.

It is often a painful subject of remark, that sometimes the very woman whose kind acts may be depended on is guilty of a serious want of kindness in her conversation; but it must be admitted that many, even of the educated in our own land,—nay, many even among Christian women,—are lamentably deficient in this respect. This we shall see, if we consider to what the law of kindness in the tongue is opposed. It is opposed to angry words. How many yield to angry passions, and utter, in unguarded moments, words which can never be recalled, and which leave a painful impression on others, not to be effaced, while they thus lay up for themselves a store of bitter remembrances! Many reproofs are given in anger, which excite in the person reproved no feeling but that of ill-will; whereas, had they been spoken wisely and gently, they might have softened the heart. Anger is a temporary madness, discomposing the spirit, and rendering it unfit either for earthly duty or heavenly communion. It is, as the proverb declares, "a snare to the soul." A person cannot pray while under its influence. How can we ask for sins to be forgiven, if we are either angry without a cause, or even on lawful causes are carrying anger too far? or who can turn, in the midst of proud and angry words, to the lowly prayer, the confession of sin, the deep humility of heart, with which alone we can approach the footstool of Jehovah? It is not before God's throne that we can indulge in wrath; and as we may at any moment be called to die, so we ought at every moment to be fit for prayer. And wrath and anger are especially sinful and displeasing in a woman, as gentleness is her especial virtue. "A man," says a female writer, "in a furious passion, is terrible to his enemies; but a woman in a passion is disgusting to her friends; she loses the respect due to her sex, and she has not masculine strength and courage to enforce any other species of respect."

There is indeed an anger which is not sinful, nor contrary to the law of kindness which should ever govern a woman's tongue. There is a righteous indignation against sin and oppression, which we find enjoined in Scripture by the words, "Be ye angry, and sin not," and which the holy apostles, and even our Saviour himself, so often expressed while on earth. Had not public anger been shown against slavery, our country might still have labored under its heavy guilt, and our fellow-creatures under its mighty curse. Against this, as against other national and individual sins, woman's voice was not wanting to express displeasure, nor was woman's hand slow to aid the great philanthropists who sought its extinction. So, in private life, warm and indignant words against wrong and guilt, so far from offending God, are often marked by his approbation, as proofs of that deep feeling of right, and that moral courage, for which the holy woman of the text was commended by the pen of inspiration.

The apostle James, whose epistle contains more admonitions against the sins of the tongue than can be found in any other portion of Holy Writ, has said, "The tongue is a fire, a world of iniquity: so is the tongue among our members, that it defileth the whole body, and setteth on fire the course of nature, and it is set on fire of hell." O! beautiful on woman's lips is the law of kindness, turning away wrath by a soft answer; bearing with the irritabilities or the infirmities of others, who have had fewer advantages in early training; enforcing truth with gentleness and persuasion, and uttering that love which is described by St. Paul as that which "beareth all things, believeth all things, hopeth all things, and endureth all things."

But far more commonly, among women in general, is the law of kindness violated by censoriousness, or by sarcastic remark, than by anger. This sin of the tongue is peculiar to neither sex, but is one which prevails to a great extent in female society. The peculiar faculties of women, as well as their habits, make this an offence against which they ought to be watchful. In them exist a quickness of perception and imagination, and consequently a ready sense of the ludicrous; and these, combined with a facility of speech, a power of detail, and often a great degree of leisure, expose them to the temptation of indulging in that "evil speaking" which God's word has commanded us to put far away from us. The habit of censuring the absent has much in it which ought to be offensive to every generous mind. "Thou shalt not speak evil of the deaf," is one of the commands of the law of Moses, which appeals to every right sentiment; yet the same principle might be carried further, and lead us to avoid speaking ill of the absent.

Nor is censoriousness chargeable only on those who strive to exaggerate the reports of evil which they may have heard, or who put on them the worst possible construction. To a sin like this surely Christian women cannot be addicted; but many, alas! are not exempt from the habit of dwelling, in conversation, on the actual faults and follies of others. Few seem to think it is a sin, yet it is decidedly opposed to the law of kindness that should regulate the tongue. It is a practice, too, which increases by indulgence.

It may begin by an expression of displeasure against vice, but soon advances to a watchfulness for offences in others. If we are to make a man an offender for a word, if we are to watch narrowly for his faults, it is generally easy enough to find some cause of censure. In many things we offend all; and few indeed are they who can be found always exempt from the blame of censoriousness. But when we are speaking of the faults of our neighbor, we are sinning against love. And how many are the reputations which have been injured by the repetition of casual remarks! Well might the Hebrew sage declare, that "life and death are in the power of the tongue;" for unkind remarks, and unjust suspicions, have sometimes subjected the sensitive to griefs more distressing than even death itself.

"O! never, never let us fling
The barb of woe to wound another;
O! never let us haste to bring
The cup of sorrow to a brother."

And who are they who are foremost to detect the faults of others, and to judge them severely? Certainly not those who have watched most diligently over their own hearts. They who have striven and longed most for conformity to the law of God, and to the example of the Saviour, know best how many graces need diligent cultivation, how many sins need to be subdued. They know, too, that often, when they have believed that some sin had been conquered, it has, in an unguarded hour, again given them sorrow, and again they have had to pray for help, and to strive against it. And ever has it been seen that the best and holiest are the most pitiful; and that they who have the law of kindness on the tongue are the very women who are most likely also to open the mouth with wisdom, and to live in the consistent practice of every feminine duty.

And the sarcastic reply, too, how frequently does it wound! If others sin, we are not to let that sin pass unnoticed. "Thou shalt in any wise rebuke thy brother, and not suffer sin upon him." But in what way is reproof to be administered? We are told to rebuke with all long-suffering and gentleness. Sin is a deep evil; it is not to be spoken of lightly, nor to be the subject of a bitter jest. It is to engage our earnest expostulation. The apostle spoke, even weeping, of those who were enemies to the cross of Christ; and with a conviction of our sinful nature, and our dependence on the grace of God for safety, we are to reprove others. Sarcasm should never be on the lip of a Christian woman, for she, indeed, should ever be found with the law of kindness on her tongue. If bitterness is in the word of reproof, the reprover is not sinless; and her rebuke does not originate from the love of God, and the hatred of sin, but from the indulgence of a sinful nature. Pride must not be met by pride pride in others is never cured by being mortified and insulted, but is rather increased into hatred and revenge. Wherefore, putting away all wrath and malice, and evil speaking, "be kindly affectioned one to another."

The law of kindness is often broken, also, by haughty words spoken to inferiors, when, forgetful that the dependant is one of God's large family, he is addressed as a stranger and an alien. The haughty look and the proud heart are an abomination unto the Lord. Pride ever proceeds, too, from an ignorance of ourselves, as Wordsworth has said:

> "He who feels contempt for any living thing
> Has faculties within his soul which he has never used;
> And thought with him is in its infancy."

Who has not marked the mild and blessed influence of her on whose tongue is the law of kindness? It is to such a woman that the little child comes for direction. It is to such that the sufferer tells his tale of sorrow, in full certainty of that ready sympathy which can do so much to lessen it; and whether the tale be that of bodily pain, or of the deeper woe of mental emotion; whether it be of the convinced spirit struggling with a sense of sin, and with only a vague idea of the possibility of pardon, or perhaps with no idea at all ; or whether it be some temporary cause of depression, some worldly loss, or some unexpected unkindness,—yet all may be soothed by the gentle accents of compassion and tenderness. How many quarrels are averted by the mediation and counsel of such a woman! how many beginnings of strife stopped in their progress by a word of gentle remonstrance! and how many little domestic troubles prevented or met by her kindly warning or encouragement! And let no woman say that she cannot acquire a sweet temper ; that she cannot always have on her lips the law of kindness. She may be naturally irritable, and, worse still, her natural irritability may never have been checked by the restraining power of early education ; but there is a deeper and fuller restraining influence than even that,—namely, the principle of love to God ; and the cultivation of this love in the heart will lead to a prayer for holiness of heart and lip, which never goes up to Heaven unanswered, and to a constant and earnest striving with a besetting sin, which God's Holy Spirit will aid and bless.

SECTION XVIII.

SHE LOOKETH WELL TO THE WAYS OF HER HOUSEHOLD, AND EATETH NOT THE BREAD OF IDLENESS.

Knowing, as we do, the great influence which family training has on the world at large, we cannot wonder that he who divided mankind into families should so commend the woman who looked well to the ways of those who compose the circle which she superintends. The constant recognition of family duties, the express injunctions that women should be keepers at home, and love their husbands and their children, all lead us to the remembrance that God is not only the God of individuals, but that he is indeed the God of families. It was the praise given of the patriarch, by Jehovah, "I know Abraham, that he will command his household after him." Moses reminded the ancient Hebrew that the statutes of God were not for himself only, but that "they were for his son's son, all the days of his life;" and added to his

She

LOOKETH WELL TO THE WAYS
OF HER HOUSEHOLD,
AND EATETH NOT THE
BREAD OF IDLENESS.

command the assurance "that it may be well with thee, and with thy children after thee." The Great Founder of human families knew that it could be well with the people in general only in proportion as household duty and religion were taught and practised. From the house, the quiet hearth, and the peaceful vine-arbor, were to go forth those who should form the future nation. And still the senator and the philosopher, the philanthropist and the missionary, go from the house of youth full of the sentiments which they have learned there, and with their habits formed on the model of home.

There is something so endearing in the ties which weave around the early home, that every human heart feels their power. The gentle words of a mother's love, the counsels of a father's wisdom, how do they return with freshness and vividness upon the spirit, long after the lips which uttered them have mingled with the dust; and are awakened with all their power by some little incident, some casual word, the sight of a handwriting, the scent of a flower. The Rev. James Hamilton records the narrative of one who unexpectedly joined with a family in the solemn service of family prayer; one who had wandered from God and truth, yet was recalled to religion and duty by this circumstance. And was it the word of God, as uttered in that prayer, which subdued the proud spirit of infidelity? No! he heard it not; his heart was filled with the remembrances of home. He thought of the peaceful hearth on which his own father once knelt, and commended to God his surrounding family. All the guilt which he had incurred by his forgetfulness of the prayers and lessons of home rushed upon his spirit, and from that hour he sought the God of his fathers.

And who has never felt a deep emotion at the thought of the home of his youth? The child at school yearns for his home; the sailor on the deep is full of thoughts of that one happy spot of earth; and when the angry waves threaten his bark, his heart swells with the remembrance of home. The prodigal who wilfully left that home is often led back to the paths of virtue and religion, as some of its teachings are brought to his mind. And the exile, and the weary wanderer,—is not home to them so dear, as that they cannot name it but with a trembling breath? and as the moon smiles out on the scene of their exile, does not the recollection that she smiles too on their home bow down even the strong man, and bring tears into the eyes of those who are little used to weep? And the wanderer on this world's wilderness, who has found that earth has no home for him,—can any sweeter description be given to him, or one which speaks more touchingly to his heart of a future world, than this, "There remaineth therefore a rest to the people of God,"—a home never to change,—a mansion that passeth not away?

When God gives to a mother's care a helpless child, what a solemn charge does the mother receive! A being born for eternity, a creature destined to everlasting happiness or misery, is committed to her, and its future character and destiny in great measure dependent on her instruction and example—its eternal condition often determined by the hours spent in the home of its parents. And God has given great encouragement to the mother who looks well to the ways of her household; for when he says, "Train up a child in the way he should go," he adds the promise, "and when he is old he will not depart from it." This promise has often been fulfilled in the holy and useful lives of those whose home has proved a nursery for God. And though the child of a pious mother may stray in youth from the ways of wisdom, yet often he returns to the path of truth before he is old. And when we see the child of religious parents wandering on in error and vice, and at last dying impenitent, shall we conclude that the promise of God has failed? Alas! it is not every pious mother who looks well to the ways of her household. The love of the creature sometimes overpowers for a time the love of the Creator; and, as in the case of the sons of Eli, the child is too often left to his uncontrolled passions, and the mother, in helpless sorrow, looks on the growth of vices which it was her duty to check, and drinks at last, with bitter anguish, the cup which her own mismanagement and indulgence had filled. She can value and keep God's word herself, but has not courage to command her children, or to make them obey.

Nor is it only while the child forms one of his parents' household, that there is a danger of failing in the duty of training him rightly. Many a pious parent fulfils to the children under his roof the command given to God's ancient people when Moses said, "These words, which I command thee this day, shall be in thine heart; and thou shalt teach them diligently unto thy children, and shalt talk of them when thou sittest in thine house, and when thou walkest by the way, and when thou liest down, and when thou risest up." But ambition and the love of the world, which seemed to have been stifled in the parent's heart for himself, are sometimes awakened for his child. He may have seemed to learn the lesson of being content with lowly things, but is tempted to seek great things for his children. How often do we see this when a child is sent forth from his own home! Some school, eminent for the learning and accomplishments of its instructor, is preferred to that in which piety forms the basis of education. Some eligible appointment presents itself. Some means of increasing riches, some opportunity of forming connections which may be of use in advancing his progress in the world, is offered; and the child, trained in his parents' household to the duties of religion and virtue, is sent into the world, at an age when his character is unformed, into scenes of great danger. And then come the bitter consequences. The youth forgets the coun sels of wisdom; he stifles the voice of conscience; and the pleasures of the world allure him. Perhaps he loses his morality, or even if his outward conduct remains the same, yet spiritual religion gradually loses its influence; and the very mother who in early life looked diligently to his ways, has perhaps joined her efforts in sending him thus unshielded into the world.

The looking well to the ways of her household includes also the care of domestic servants; and the maidens to whom the Jewish matron gave their portion of food and work were doubtless guarded from evil by her watchful prudence. Some mistresses appear to think that little responsibility attaches to them with regard to servants, and that so long as they provide them with home, and food, and wages, they perform all the duty required. But the ways of every member of a household should be looked to by her whom Providence has placed at the head of a family. The habits of life, the moral and religious character of each, should be regarded by the mistress; and if an ignorant servant becomes a member of a household, she should be instructed. It is plainly the duty of all to lead a useful life, and it is in the immediate circle that we are to commence our labors. The mistress of a family, while remembering that her own advantages of training may have been superior to those placed under her care, should strive that every servant who enters her dwelling should be benefited during her residence there. Especially she should employ the means of restraint with which she is endowed by her authority, to prevent any irregularity of conduct, and the practice of any wrong habits. She should see to the ways of her household, by taking care that every one composing it should attend to the means of religion. Time and opportunity should be given for serving God. Her authority should keep them from scenes of vice and dissipation, and from evil company; and, in forming her domestic plans, it is hers to regulate both their comfort and their duty, on the broad principle of Christian benevolence: "Whatsoever ye would that others should do unto you, do ye also unto them."

It is desirable for the comfort of a family, and for its permanent welfare, that the servants should be rightly directed and kindly treated. Such con duct meets its immediate reward. Children are necessarily influenced by them, and in that respect the character of servants is most important to every household. In every family in which they are kept, their performance of duty is requisite for order and comfort, and this must be determined by their moral character. Their willing service, and even their thoughtful tenderness, are required in the hour of sickness, and their sympathy and help is sometimes wanted in the day of sorrow. During that awful season of tragic suffering comprised in the French revolution, many valuable lives were saved by the attachment of confidential servants; and that period, remarkable for the exhibition of some of the deepest crimes and some of the sweetest virtues of human nature, presents a record of devoted men and maidens, who counted not even their own lives dear unto them, so that they might rescue from danger some mistress whose former kindness had cheered them, or some helpless child whom they once had carried in their arms. The history of the church of God, too, could present details of holy and useful servants, from the time when Phœbe was a servant at Cenchrea, and Onesimus was dear to the apostle Paul, to the recent days when the Dairyman's Daughter performed her humble duties with exalted faith and fervent piety. till her spirit sought its heavenly home, and her frame was laid in its lowly grave.

A woman so well taught in wisdom's ways as the matron of the text, would know well that idleness leads certainly to vice and sorrow. Idleness and fulness of bread were the vices mentioned as exciting God's wrath against the sinful Sodom, and were doubtless the chief means of fostering all its depravity. It is, indeed, the source of a thousand ills, and so certain a cause of discomfort, that happier is he who earns his bread by the sweat of his brow, than he who spends his life in indolence. Cheerfulness is almost the necessary result of moderate employment, just as *ennui* and languor are the consequences of a life without pursuit. "Idleness," says old Burton, somewhat quaintly, "is the badge of gentry; the bane of body and mind; the nurse of naughtiness; the step-mother of discipline; the chief author of all mischief; one of the seven deadly sins; the cushion on which the devil chiefly reposes; and a great cause, not only of melancholy, but of many other diseases; for the mind is naturally active, and if it be not occupied about some honest business, it rushes into mischief, or sinks into melancholy."

And what woman would wish so to pass her life that at death she should not be missed? Of how many might it be said that the world and the home could well spare them; but who can tell the worth of a life spent in useful occupation? It is not till the seat is vacant on which the busy matron sat,—it is not till the implements of industry lie by unused, till the animating voice is silent, and the busy hand is still,—that we fully perceive how much was done hourly, and quietly, and surely, in the well-regulated home. From many such a hearth, when the mother has been taken, the comfort of home is gone too; and ill-managed children, once so tenderly cared for, show their orphan condition to every passer by. There is a solemn responsibility attaching to life,—a responsibility only to be met by active exertion; and a woe is denounced against the idle. A woman who looked well to the ways of her household would not only herself avoid eating the bread of idleness, but she would see that each one had a suitable engagement; and every one who is the mother of a family not compelled to work, should strive to interest her children in some one employment which they should cultivate with pleasure, and which should call forth their latent energies. Much may be done for the young, by consulting their tastes, and encouraging them in some pursuit; and the skill to select this does not require in the mother so much talent, as the exertion of that tact which is so common to women, and which, like many other faculties, is rendered stronger by a woman's affection.

One of the first aims of education should be to promote activity of mind; and the acquisition of a taste for simple and unexpensive pleasures is, in itself, so valuable a source of enjoyment, that it is to be regretted that this is also not made a more usual part of education. On this account, may be recommended the study of the various departments of natural history and science. It may seem to matter little, indeed, that a woman should be a botanist, or an entomologist, though all would allow that these pursuits might afford much pleasure; but the activity of mind, and the power of application and observation, which such a study will awaken, is of incalculable worth. Plutarch said that a woman who studied geometry would not be fond of dancing; and we may add, that a woman who feels interested in studies of this nature will neither be frivolous nor idle.

But it is only to the few that the choice of the pursuits of life is left. The many are called to work in this anxious, toiling world, and thousands are sighing for that leisure which others waste so carelessly. But has active and regular employment no advantages? Does not the heart fill with pleasure, when the eye marks the fruit of exertion; and does not the hour of occasional recreation bring with it far more of enjoyment, and is it not fuller of life, than is the day of indolence to the unemployed? Above all, is not the busy man or woman living the life which God has ordained? His own word has said, "If any will not work, neither shall he eat." The ancient Hebrews had all their occupations. The rich and the poor were alike taught in the knowledge of some business, by which they might labor with hand or head; nor did rank or station exempt any from useful toil. And the result of this industry was a thoughtful and provilent people; a nation standing out from oriental nations generally, as marked by an energy and force of character, much of which has descended to the modern Jew, under all the varied circumstances of place and time.

In the consideration of the Christian graces, one cannot help remarking that they are all active. Piety is not to consist in quiet contemplation, but in active duty. If we read in the Scripture of love, then there is the labor of love; and every kind heart knows the truth of the proverb, that love can make labor light. If we read of faith, it is of an active faith,—a work of faith,—a faith which overcometh the world. If of hope, then is it a hope powerful enough to expel sin, since he who hath this hope purifieth himself, even as God is pure. Holy principle must lead to holy practice; and the woman who, while professing to serve God, neglects the duty of caring for her household, dishonors her Christian profession, and brings disgrace upon God's cause. Even the Great Creator of the universe himself is represented as active. Our Saviour remarked, "My Father worketh hitherto, and I work." Our blessed Lord lived a life of unwearied labor in the cause of man. The angels, too, are represented as employed, not only in tuning their harps of gold and singing the songs of the celestial city, but as winging their way to this world on ministries of love; and who shall say how much they who shall be heirs of salvation are indebted to their guardian care?

"Where burns the loved hearth brightest,
  Cheering the social breast?
Where beats the fond heart lightest,
  Its humble hopes possessed?
Where is the smile of sadness,
  Of meek-eyed patience born,
Worth more than those of gladness,
  Which mirth's bright cheek adorn?
Pleasure is marked by fleetness
  To those who ever roam,
While grief itself has sweetness
  At Home, DEAR HOME!"

HER

CHILDREN ARISE UP,
AND CALL HER BLESSED;
HER HUSBAND ALSO,
AND HE PRAISETH HER.

SECTION XIX.

HER CHILDREN ARISE UP AND CALL HER BLESSED: HER HUSBAND ALSO, AND HE PRAISETH HER.

Very probably the expression of rising up to bless the parent may have some allusion to the eastern practice of rising and bowing to the ground before the head of the family, as this mode of reverence is very general. Yet it will bear the meaning in which it would be taken in our land,—that the children rise from infancy to childhood, and on to youth and manhood, with hearts full of affection, and grateful recollections of the worth of an excellent mother.

It has been said that home praise is the truest praise; certainly none can know us so well as those who surround the family hearth. A far higher virtue and more consistent excellence belongs to her of whom all her household can speak well, than to those who shine only in company, and who require but the charms of politeness and the graces of conversation to gain approval. And how pleasant is it to hear the blessings bestowed by the child on the name of the good mother! Who shall tell the hours of anxiety, the words of care and tenderness, which such a mother has bestowed on his infancy; the sleepless nights, and careful days, and all the maternal solicitudes, which shielded from harm his childhood and early youth; and which, as he grew older, changed their mode of expression, but never lost sight of their object? Truly did Gray say, "We can never have but one mother." No love, not even the tenderest, can equal hers; for she will love on, though sickness should wither the flower and turn all its beauty into decay; and fix her firmest and deepest affection on that one of her children who has least of outward grace and loveliness. Her love, unlike all others, can withstand neglect, and ingratitude, and forgetfulness. The prodigal son may stray from his home, and the world may frown on him, and frown justly; and all the love of neighbors, or of friends, or even of brother or sister, may have been worn out by his folly and wickedness; yet is there a stream of love in the mother's heart, ever fresh and ever living; he is still her own loved son; and one word of penitence, one look of sorrow, will win forgiveness for a life of unkindness. The love of a mother is like the bounty of God, who "causeth his sun to rise on the evil and on the good, and sendeth rain on the just and on the unjust."

It is, indeed, a sure proof of their excellent education, when all the children of a family can arise and call their mother blessed. And when all are gathered in the circle of love, such a home presents the loveliest scene on earth.

> "Domestic Happiness, thou only bliss
> Of Paradise that has survived the fall!
> Though few now taste thee, unimpaired and pure;
> Or, tasting, long enjoy thee; too infirm
> Or too incautious to preserve thy sweets
> Unmixed with drops of bitter, which neglect
> Or temper sheds into thy crystal cup.
> Thou art the nurse of Virtue; — in thine arms
> She smiles, appearing, as in truth she is,
> Heaven-born, and destined to the skies again."

When the law was given from Mount Sinai to ancient Israel, we find included in it not only the reverence of the father, but "Thou shalt honor thy father and thy mother," was its direct injunction. It would be from the lip of his mother that the Jewish child would learn his most sacred lessons. It must be remembered that the young Israelite had no school but his home. He was not sent away from the paternal roof to gather learning; but under its happy shadow he learned, from his parents' lips, his knowledge of business, of life and duty, and became early familiar with the law of God. He had not, perhaps, even his smaller Bible to refer to, but this law was taught in the house when the family met together; it was written up upon the gates of the city, and read aloud by the priests and Levites to assembled multitudes. It does not seem that, previous to the Babylonish captivity, the ancient Israelites had schools, save those for the "sons of the prophets,"—the pious youths who were destined to be teachers in Israel;—but many a mother's tongue could tell of Israel's Hope, the glorious Messiah, the Prince of the people, for whom every devout Israelite was hoping and looking; and for whose advent the Hebrew matron was so anxious, that she grieved if she was childless, because she hoped that from her house might spring forth the "Prophet like unto Moses." Guided by his mother's hand, the Jewish child went to the temple, which God had chosen. From her lip he learned the meaning of those yearly festivals, when every male among the Jews appeared in Jerusalem, the holy city; and when, in after times, they sang, as they went up, that beautiful Psalm,—"I was glad when they said unto me, Let us go into the house of the Lord. Our feet shall stand within thy gates, O Jerusalem. Jerusalem is builded as a city that is compact together: whither the tribes go up, the tribes of the Lord, unto the testimony of Israel, to give thanks unto the name of the Lord." And thus the pious Hebrew mother would weave with her child's earliest impressions a store of associations to bless his after years. O that every mother in our own land would make her home a nursery for God; and teach such Christian principle, and enjoin such Christian practice, as would fully insure her children's love! Then of every American mother might it be said, "Her children arise up, and call her blessed."

The husband of the excellent woman is represented as adding his praise to that of the younger members of the family. He could indeed point to her example for their imitation. He could praise her, not alone for the comfort which her useful energy cast throughout his home, but for the sweetness which her gentleness and goodness brought into it, and which rendered it so attractive. He could tell of enjoyment provided by her industry; of anxieties prevented by her caution; of sorrows lightened by her sympathy; and could perhaps look around on children walking in the fear of the Lord, who learned that fear from the teaching of their mother.

"O, say to mothers what a holy charge
Is theirs!—with what a kingly power their love
Might rule the fountain of the new-born mind!
Warn them to wake at early dawn, and sow
Good seed before the world hath sown her tares;
Nor in their toil decline, that angel bands
May put their sickle in, and reap for God,
And gather to his garner."

MANY

DAUGHTERS HAVE DONE
VIRTUOUSLY, BUT
THOU EXCELLEST THEM ALL.

SECTION XX.

MANY DAUGHTERS HAVE DONE VIRTUOUSLY, BUT THOU EXCELLEST THEM ALL.

Judging from probabilities, we can hardly suppose that this high commendation is intended to be taken by the inspired writer as the praise given by God to the Jewish matron. Commentators generally refer to the warm expression of affection and esteem uttered either by her husband or children, on a review of her consistent and valuable life. Nor was this expression of an overflowing affection without justice or truth; for one who acted so well would far exceed in virtue the generality of wives and mothers, and would probably be superior in worth to any woman known by those who praised her. The Septuagint, Syriac, and other versions render this passage, "Many daughters have gathered riches;" and as industry seems to have been a ruling feature in the character of Hebrew women generally at this early period, this rendering would not be unsuitable. In such case, the praise would extend not only to the number of garments which she had wrought for merchandise, but to her skill in acquiring property, and her care in preventing an unnecessary expenditure of wealth.

But although so finished a degree of excellence as that recorded in this beautiful poem must, at any period of this world's history, have been a rare attainment, yet a great degree of loveliness and virtue marked many of the women of early days. To all the mental vigor, and industry, and noble sentiments, which belong to the matron of ancient Rome, the Jewish female seems to have added a warm, enthusiastic, and gentle tenderness, which renders her lovelier than the sterner Roman lady; and which, while it commands our respect, wins a deeper and warmer love. Nor was the Hebrew woman wanting in that clear intellect, or versatility of talent, which fitted her for rivalling the Grecian dame in the lighter and more graceful accomplishments of life. The commands of Moses, the writings of the prophets,—nay, the very history of the creation of the world, on which the eye of the ancient Israelite pondered,— all taught that woman was not intended for the slave of man. Recognizing the woman as an immortal being, providing for her protection and comfort, giving to her, as to her husband, the assurances of God's favor and the hopes of a future life, presenting her to the Hebrew as the mother of the coming Messiah, the Jewish woman was raised above that degradation to which the oriental female was subjected ; and still, even in Asia, enjoys a freedom and an importance unknown among other Asiatics. "The singular beauty of the Hebrew women," says an interesting writer, "and the natural warmth of their affections, have conspired to throw gems of domestic loveliness over the pages of the Bible. In no history can there be found a greater number of charming female portraits. From Hagar, down to Mary and Martha, the Bible presents pictures of womanly beauty that are unsurpassed and rarely paralleled. But we should very imperfectly represent, in these general remarks, the formative influence of the female character as seen in the Bible, did we not refer these amiable traits of character to the original conceptions of which we have spoken, and to the pure and lofty religious ideas which the American books in general present. If woman, then, appears as the companion and friend of man, if she rises to that noble position which is held by the mother of a family, she owes her elevation in the main to the religion of Moses and to that of Jesus. The first system, as a preparatory one, did not, and could not, complete the emancipation of woman." Let American females remember what Christianity has done for them, and that their responsibility is consequently greatly increased.

"Charms there may be, that waken admiration
When first beheld, that have no dwelling-place
On memory's tablet; while on it we trace
Features less perfect, and less marked at first,
But made indelible by softer grace;
Too unobtrusive all at once to burst
Upon the gazer's soul, — once known, forever nursed
With cherished fondness, for the much-loved sake
Of purest happiness, which these alone
Have had the power within our hearts to wake,
By witchery peculiarly their own."

FAVOR

IS DECEITFUL, AND BEAUTY IS VAIN; BUT A WOMAN THAT FEARETH THE LORD, SHE SHALL BE PRAISED.

SECTION XXI.

FAVOR IS DECEITFUL, AND BEAUTY IS VAIN; BUT A WOMAN THAT FEARETH THE LORD, SHE SHALL BE PRAISED.

Little do we need a revelation to tell us that worldly favor is vain indeed: experience of the world attests it; and the philosopher, and still more frequently the poet, have again and again lamented the worthlessness of the favor of this world. For a little while, the man who rises in general favor is loved and honored, his presence welcomed, his opinion valued; but soon some new favorite takes his place, and general adulation is directed to the rising sun. How many have sickened, as they told how in hours of prosperity the smile of the rich and the praise of the young and the gay were given for a season; and then, as some new mood came over the public mind, they were left to die in poverty; while they who once sought their society looked at them now with cold indifference, and passed by them as strangers.

But the instability of worldly favor is not confined to public praise; for, in the more private circles of fashionable life, it is equally deceitful Favor is given to a woman because she is rich, or beautiful, or elegant. She is praised and admired, and learns to take such admiration as her right; and she finds it a true proverb, that "Men will praise thee when thou doest well to thyself." But poverty comes suddenly, even as an armed man; sickness overtakes her, and all her beauty fades like that of the flower of the field; and the graces, which gave life and spirit to the gay assembly, are gone forever. Then she can add hers to the sad testimony of the poet·

> "The friends who in our sunshine live,
> When winter comes are flown;
> And she who hath but tears to give,
> Must weep those tears alone."

How frequently does the young and trusting heart swell with emotion, on the discovery of the deceitful nature of worldly favor! "The greetings where no kindness is" are taken by the truthful as truth itself; and when they change to coldness or contempt, the ardent spirit shrinks beneath them, as the lily withers when the sunshine of heaven changes to the chill north wind. And the young, having no hope of God's favor, or of happiness in the world to come, exchange for a misanthropic and ungentle spirit the trusting affection of an ingenuous mind, and become like the cold and worldly beings whose deceitful favor once misled them.

Perhaps there is scarcely a woman who has not listened to the voice of flattery; and though the coarse praise of a flattering tongue would disgust the pious, and displease too the cultivated and refined, yet most have been sometimes beguiled by its more delicate and skilful application. There is a self-love in every human heart to which such praise can appeal; and even the woman who knows the commendation to be undeserved will sometimes be pleased, as she believes that such at least is the opinion of those who utter it. But time comes, and truth comes with him, and with rude hand tears away the veil from falsehood, and the deceived spirit learns at length the lesson that favor is deceitful.

And is Christian intercourse altogether free from

this deceitfulness? Are there not prevalent, in Christian society, words and practices which express far more than the heart can respond to? To the courtesies of life no Christian should be indifferent. If the worldly woman learns, from the politeness of the world, to prefer the comfort of others to her own,—if she must make sacrifices of feeling, that in society she may appear kind and polite,—how much more should Christian women practise a gentle courtesy of manner, from the consideration that even Christ pleased not himself. "Be ye kind, be ye courteous," is the injunction of a holy apostle; and all rudeness and incivility should be shunned by every woman professing to have been taught of God.

On the other hand, is not the favor of that woman deceitful, who stretches out the hand of kindness to her acquaintance, who welcomes her to her house, and listens with apparent sympathy to the expression of her feelings,—and who will, on her absence, recount her faults or ridicule her follies? O that all Christian women were wholly free from this portion of worldly false-heartedness, this conformity to worldly favor; and were ever sincere and candid in their expressions of friendship! On them, at least, let the trusting heart lean, in full assurance that the love which is uttered is the love which is felt.

But while we must admit that, even in Christian intercourse, much imperfection exists, and the spirit of the world sometimes darkens the brighter lustre of the Christian character, yet it has ever been the lot of the sorrowful and desolate to find compassion and sincerity nowhere so fully developed as in the circle of those who are the real followers of Christ. The woman who sincerely fears the Lord, who lives nearest to him, will be, too, the truest and best of earthly friends; and when David said, "I am a companion of all them that fear thee," he could number among those servants of God the faithful friends of his hours of adversity; and he could think of the pleasant Jonathan, and the liberal Barzillai, and the faithful Nathan,—men who never forsook him when sorrow came, whose favor was never deceitful; but who loved him best when most he needed their friendship, because their love was strengthened by their fear and love of God.

And are not the favor and love of God unchanging? He has said, "Call upon me in the day of trouble;" he has bid us, when earthly favor has proved deceitful, to bring the worn and weary spirit to him for refuge. And no one ever sought him in vain, or had reason to regret that he had cast all his care on the loving-kindness of an unchanging God.

We have not need to look far to see the passing nature, the vanity, of personal beauty:

> "For not a year but pilfers, as it goes,
> Some youthful grace that age would gladly keep:"

and time brings assuredly his wrinkles to furrow the fairest countenance. Sudden or prolonged sickness changes the rose on the cheek to paleness, and dims the eye whose brightness told a tale of health and gladness; for when God with rebukes doth chasten for iniquity, he maketh beauty to pass away like a moth; so that all, even in their best states, are altogether vanity. But the frailty of beauty is most apparent when we look on death,—on that change which all must encounter. "It is," says Jeremy Taylor, "a mighty change that is made by the death of every person, and it is visible to us who are alive. Reckon but from the sprightfulness of youth, and the fair cheeks and the full eyes of childhood; from the vigorousness and strong flexure of the joints of five-and-twenty, to the hollowness and dead paleness, to the loathsomeness and horror, of a three days' burial, and he shall perceive the distance to be very great and very strange."

"O, what is beauty's power?
It perishes and dies.
Shall the cold earth its silence break,
To tell how soft and smooth a cheek
Beneath its surface lies?
Mute, mute is all,
O'er beauty's fall;
Her praise resounds no more when mantled in her pall."

"But a woman that feareth the Lord, she shall be praised." Such a woman would have praise of God. The ornament of a meek and quiet spirit is of great price, and to the true believer in Christ God will say, at the great day, "Well done, good and faithful servant; enter thou into the joy of thy Lord." And, O! what praise can equal this? Men may praise those whom God disapproves. They may hold that to be good which God abhors; and even when they have the right standard of holiness, yet they may so little know the hearts of others as to mistake in their estimate of good and evil. On whom is the praise of men bestowed? On those who conquer kingdoms, who perform great exploits in discovery and science, who make high attainments in knowledge, or who clothe in lofty verse thoughts of beauty and genius. And who will deny his meed of praise to the philosopher or the poet? We owe them so much, that we could not pluck a leaf from the laurel or the bay, without ingratitude. Yet, in all their thoughts of sublimity or tenderness, there may be no fear of God; he may not be pleased. "To that man will I look," saith Jehovah, "who is of an humble and contrite heart, and who trembleth at my word." The humble and lowly Christian, performing the simplest and commonest duties of domestic life in his fear; seeking his counsel, and earnestly striving to keep his commands; praying for the guidance of the Holy Spirit, and confidently trusting for the pardon of her sin in him who died on the cross to redeem her,—this is the woman on whom shall be bestowed that best, that only praise which is truly valuable; for of her the Lord himself shall say, "She hath chosen that good part, which shall not be taken away from her."

GIVE HER OF THE FRUIT OF HER HANDS, AND LET HER OWN WORKS PRAISE HER IN THE GATES.

SECTION XXII.

GIVE HER OF THE FRUIT OF HER HANDS; AND LET HER OWN WORKS PRAISE HER IN THE GATES.

Questions have been raised whether this passage is a continuation of the praise bestowed on this excellent matron by her husband, or whether it may not be regarded as a prayer offered up on her behalf. We have spoken of the gate as the place of assembly and of commerce, where the fruits of her industry would be known and appreciated, and where men would speak of her virtues; where she would be mentioned as a great example of female excellence, and her deeds of mercy and her unblamable life would characterize her as a mother in Israel, and a devout and humble servant of the great Jehovah.

Although a life of consistent virtue generally brings its own reward in the esteem of all whose opinion is truly valuable, and though the hand of the diligent usually, in some degree, maketh rich, yet it is not always in this world that the good receive of the fruit of their hands. But there is a world on which the holy women of old have long since entered, — a world to which we are all hastening, — when every one shall receive according to the deeds done in the body, whether they be good, or whether they be evil. We cannot be saved by an exemplary and virtuous life; for never yet was there a human being who lived and sinned not; and the holiest action ever performed by sinful man had yet mingled with it so much infirmity of motive, that it needed the atoning blood of Christ to render it acceptable in the eyes of an infinitely holy God. But Christian principle, though it will not enable us, while in this world, to offer a perfect obedience, will certainly be accompanied by the practice of holiness, an earnest endeavor after godliness, and a hatred and avoidance of sin. For the Scripture has said, "As the body without the spirit is dead, so faith without works is dead also." While we cannot answer God for one of a thousand of our transgressions, yet he will reward the humblest deed of good which proceeds from love to Christ. And when the beloved apostle spoke of the blessedness of those who die in the Lord, he adds, "They rest from their labors, and their works do follow them." The pious deeds which they had wrought on earth were not forgotten in heaven; but they followed as evidences of love to Christ, as the result of holy principles, and are thus accepted and approved by a gracious God. Blessed indeed are they who steadily endure, amid all temptation; for when they are tried, they shall receive the crown of life, which the Lord hath promised to them that love him; and thus the fruits of their hands and hearts shall be given to them through all eternity.

"O! in our sterner manhood, when no ray
Of earlier sunshine glimmers on our way, —
When girt with sin, and sorrow, and the toil
Of cares which tear the bosom that they soil, —
O! if there be in retrospection's chain
One link that knits us with young dreams again,
One thought so sweet we scarcely dare to muse
On all the hoarded raptures it reviews,
Which seems each instant, in its backward range,
The heart to soften, and its ties to change,
And every spring, untouched for years, to move,
It is — THE MEMORY OF A MOTHER'S LOVE!"

CPSIA information can be obtained
at www.ICGtesting.com
Printed in the USA
LVHW110814120522
718525LV00003B/89

9 783375 003678